MW01100412

THE ORIGIN OF VERMILION

Katy Masuga

Katy Masuga (signature)

katymasuga.weebly.com

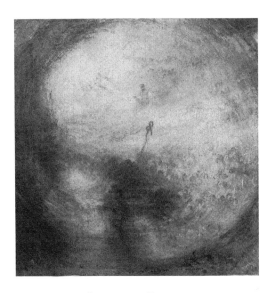

SPUYTEN DUYVIL
New York City

©2016 Katy Masuga
ISBN 978-1-941550-78-6

Cover image: *Light and Colour (Goethe's Theory) – The Morning after the Deluge – Moses Writing the Book of Genesis (1843)*
J. M. W. Turner

Library of Congress Cataloging-in-Publication Data

Masuga, Katy, 1975-
The origin of vermilion / Katy Masuga.
pages ; cm
ISBN 978-1-941550-78-6
I. Title.
PS3613.A81996O75 2016
813'.54--dc23
2015032094

To my daughters, Mullain and Rainer

Book I

Book II

BOOK I

CAPTAIN JANUARY I

Gramps lived in the chicken coop out behind the house and the barn behind the outhouse and near the pond with the ducks and the weeds. He lived there starting after gram died, and he went there because Eva came, just like when ma died and pa got rid of the chickens. Gramps lived there, and he had to bend down when he went inside to go to sleep, but I didn't have to bend down, well not that much, when I went to visit him. It was a fine place to live, he said, and I thought it was fine too, and I would come see him straight after school before even going home first with my sisters like they did. Pa thought it was fine that I spent the evenings with gramps, but Eva didn't like it so much, and I didn't like her so much anyway, and so that was alright.

The ground was cold and hard inside made of the ground all packed down, dark and cool and moist, the color of chocolate with just a little milk, and gramps had a coarse bed of thick hay and an old sack used for carrying the potatoes back from town that he used for a bed and just for sitting when it wasn't yet time for sleep. We didn't have chickens anymore not since ma died, pa couldn't take care of them anymore and didn't like seeing them running around no more neither, and the chicken care that was ma's but now she's gone and that wasn't so long ago, and even then we didn't have too many chickens and so maybe if gramps wanted, he could have lived in the coop with the chickens too before they were all gone before ma died, and maybe they would have made it a little warmer too with their nice feathers. Gramps saved the stumps of the old candles that Eva threw out when they didn't fit right or look right anymore in her candle holders that she kept on the dining table, and me and gramps, we would sit by the thick orange candle light together, and I would listen to his stories, and he would sometimes drink from an old tin can full of hot black coffee looking like molasses or sometimes a bit of the booze he had brought over from Old Hodge down at the edge of town toward the mill. I never had neither, but I could smell them so strong, I think it was like if I was drinking them myself something like when he smoked his pipe and it got me to coughing and I could taste the strong tobacco in my throat and my nose.

Gramps would talk about ma just a little and he told me that I looked like her and she was a sweet baby girl, he said he would say, and she worked hard too hard, he said, and nothing too pretty can last too long, he said and I didn't know what that meant. He'd stop talking and go silent and look down at his molasses and I just watched until he came back to me eventually and smiled and we talked about something else or it was time to go back to the house to bed. Gramps would talk about gram a lot more and that was nicer and not so sad, and he talked about when they were young and would make trips once in a while into town and maybe go dancing or to watch the moving pictures at the cinema. They didn't have a lot of money, they were just the kids of dairy farmers, but gram's pa was fond of gramps, and he gave him a job and then he came to taking care of not just the cows but his land too, and gramps never let him down, and he married gram and lived there together until gram's folks died, and it's the same land we were living on all this time, and then ma died, and Eva was going to sell everything and move us into town and send us girls off to school by ourselves, and she used to say it was so she could get some culture, she said. She wanted some culture so bad, I thought she might just go crazy. She'd sometimes come back from town smelling like she picked up all the culture you could get at the perfume counter of Malley's department store.

Pa didn't let her send us away, and that was good, and I was glad. I didn't want to go to no school away from gramps, and I thought it was just fine living evenings by the candlelight and listening to him tell stories each night and carrying on just like we did, and we weren't bothering no one even if Eva still didn't get herself enough culture, but I don't know what I might have had to do with it anyway. I didn't much mind going to school just where I was, though I didn't much like it either. But I would do it if it meant I could keep coming hear gramps tell his stories. I don't know how come my sisters didn't come listen too, but they didn't, and it's just as well.

It was a warm and turned out to be a funny kind

of spring day after I had a bad dream about gramps when I came home from school and thought maybe something wasn't going right or didn't go right and was about to not go right. And I skipped past the house when my sisters ran inside like I always do, and I ran over to gramps' place like I always do that too, and I got in there, and when I didn't find him there, then I knew surely something funny was happening. But it turned out nothing too funny was happening, not that day, but that Old Hodge got his truck stuck in some mud again, and gramps was over there trying to help him out near the old mill. So I just waited, and then gramps and me, we walked back to the chicken coop together, and I said let's pretend we're pioneers discovering the wilderness for the first time, and he said OK, Shirt, all quick in his gruff but soft voice, and so we kept an eye out for wild animals and even savages and I learned from gramps what flowers we could pick to eat up for dinner and told him maybe we could build a fire from some twigs. Gramps called me Shirt and then everyone called me Shirt. He didn't like it so much that I got named after some old cousin of ours, four years older than me, that my older sister named me after that old Captain January gal on the television box or in the moving pictures or something. Well, we didn't have no television box, and I ain't never seen the moving pictures, and gramps thought I should have my own name that suits me he said, and so he said I'd be Shirt, and that suits you just like a shirt of your own, he said.

I think now that gramps and me would still be playing pioneers if I had done better when I found him in the coop that day not moving just laying there flat like maybe he was sleeping. Things were just fine, and since nothing happened that day when Old Hodge got stuck in mud, well, I wasn't thinking too much about nothing bad happening, and so when it did just the next day I think, well I guess I just didn't manage right. I had forgotten already what I felt just that day earlier and found gramps helping Old Hodge, but this day now I came home from school and I went over to gramps' and when I found him laying there not moving, I went running to the house, but surely the only ones in there were my sisters, and they didn't know nothing either. Pa wouldn't be home from the shop yet, and Eva was in town as always. I should have stayed with gramps, and I could have helped him. I should have just stayed.

That was the end right there, and I know it was my fault. And now I just don't know what. Don't know what to do, and that's just about the end of everything. He was all I ever loved.

OIDA VS. BIRDS

1.

I pulled an old book off my shelf and found it already contained a bookmarker. An old note was placed somewhere toward the beginning of *A Portrait of the Artist as a Young Man*. I'm trying to remember where and when I acquired this book, because the note most certainly is not mine. I only very infrequently buy books new, and this is nowhere near being a new book. In fact, it has margin notes throughout, scribbled in pencil but also with pink highlighter pen. The note itself is really nothing more than a receipt from a shop, a transaction that took place seven years ago. The note's instructions seem to explain why the paper is still hanging around: *Ticket client à conserver.*

Scrawled across the front of the paperback book itself is a different sort of instruction, a personal reminder: 'Xerox Joyce notes' in thick, blue ballpoint pen. You can tell that the inscriber pushed with a certain force in order to get the message clearly imprinted on the stiff paperboard. On the back of the cover is a rhombohedron in the same blue ink and the number 'IV'. Inside the cover, the word 'Beauty' has been crossed out before being finished (reading simply 'Beaut') followed by 'Beauty vs. Planes Ugly'. Below are two lines, both difficult to decipher. They seem to be identical or meant to be identical, but whereas the first line appears to read 'Oida vs. birds', the second indicates something more like 'Art vs. Nation' or perhaps 'Art vs. Belgium'. Or is it 'Art vs. Religion'? At the same time it's evident that the first line cannot possibly read 'Oida vs. birds,' as much as it seems to do so.

I'm staring at the letters as if they are going to reveal themselves to me eventually, instead of me inflicting upon them some sort of mental trick where I put them in place to make sense out of something that seems to be hiding. The same trick I unconsciously and often do when some one speaks to me, and it seems I haven't quite understood, hearing, for example: *Bay men sat high on the ocean floor* instead of *Payments at night go under the door*. A woman introduces herself to me as Clea, I hear India. The second line of text in this book cannot read 'Art vs. Nation,' but that is all I see.

In 1977 writer and theatre critic John Heilpern wrote a book he called *Conference of the Birds*, telling the story of director Peter Brook's journey into the Sahara in the early 1970s in order to create a new form of theatre that would completely distance itself from any cultural assumptions of its audience. Brook and theatre artists from the *Centre international de recherche théâtrale* performed their pieces for the native populations in Africa with whom they shared neither language nor culture. One of the pieces in their repertoire was based on the 12th century Persian poem *The Conference of the Birds* by Farid al-Din Attar. Among Brook's international troupe of actors were a young Helen Mirren and a middle-aged Yoshi Oida, better known in his native Japan. If Peter Brook's journey was a success, I cannot say, but the subsequent productions in New York and Paris clearly were. Strangely, however, this kind of success seems to directly contradict the motivation of the exercise, since audiences in both Paris and New York would for the most part share the language and culture of the performers. Nevertheless, the piece was met with a certain conventional approval.

The 12th century poem *The Conference of the Birds* tells of the journey of a large group of birds that desires to find its god or king, the one to lead them all. The birds are informed by the hoopoe bird that this king, the great single creator of all existence, is called Simorgh. Yet the birds, one by one, fall short of completing the impossibly long journey to reach Simorgh, each failing within itself differently, revealing a personal flaw that would serve as the needed exemption for giving up. Eventually, however, a small group does manage to arrive – precisely thirty birds – and yet, mistaken in their pursuit, they do not find a king as they thought they would. They find no other being, that is to say, they do not find Simorgh as they imagined, as their god, but what they find is the stark and crystalline reflection of themselves in a glorious lake.

Come you lost Atoms to your Centre draw,
And be the Eternal Mirror that you saw:

Rays that have wander'd into Darkness wide
Return and back into your Sun subside

Sufi doctrine writes that god is not separate from the world but is the spiritual and physical conglomeration of the world itself. The collective unity of all beings, externally and internally, is the source for what the birds believed to be their god. This force itself is the totality of all existence as it lives and transforms and lives again. The birds that made the journey to find themselves in their god, or rather to find god in themselves, these birds who appear to have completed the journey, complete it through the very recognition of their reflections. They are brought into this realization through their collective image as it gazes back at them. In the gesture they become the truth that was always within them.

Simorgh appears in other legends across Asia Minor and the Middle East, taking the shape of an enormous female bird with a dog's face, lion's claws and the body of thirty beautiful birds of prey made up of their colors. Simorgh is full of love and pity, nurses her young and often performs miracles or good deeds to those in her favor.

Looking at the strange scribbling inside the old book, I tempt myself to make sense of the illegible words. I secretly hope to find or somehow to learn the story of its origination but know that any attempt to locate it here in the text can only be that of my own imagination. When such clues as these exist, it's nearly impossible not to carry the inquiry even further, looking for some unreachable universe – not only the bookowner's handwriting, the hand to which it belongs and the words written, nor even their intention, but beyond all that: the life of the bookowner, the impressions made by the book, the impact, the purpose of having bought the book, the foreknowledge, the daily life events, the meals, the sunsets the licking of postage stamps the toilet the family the cost of things the old notes on Plato on taxes on Blake on the color of the sky in the summer by the sea.

I've owned the book less than a year, but I assume the notes are many years older than that. Their owner would have no knowledge of our recent events, unprecedented developments in quantum physics, intergalactic discoveries, advancements in medicine, historical hurricanes and wildfires, terrorisms at home and beyond, racial violence, gender violence, violence against women, flight catastrophes, 1,000s of forsaken refugees. The flight of birds across still moving landscapes worldwide and, finally, the upcoming beginning of a new spring, counted off by the understated hallmark of May Day. These words cannot foresee what it will never see, never have known, never been able to offer explanations, condolences, apologies.

Below the note's instructions, *Ticket Client à conserver*, there is a single phrase written presumably by the original purchaser of the book: 'the Haymarket affair.'

The Haymarket Affair is rooted to May Day, occurring on the first of May celebrating and emphasizing workers and workers' rights and, most specifically, support for the implementation of the eight-hour workday. On May 1, 1886 in Chicago, workers in support of the eight-hour workday peacefully rallied on Haymarket Square, Chicago. As the police eventually marched in to disperse the crowd, a bomb was thrown at them killing one and inciting a five-minute exchange of fire between the poorly armed workers and the police. Because of the darkness and general mayhem all around, seven more police officers were killed by friendly fire, as well as an unknown number of civilians. The trial of eight alleged anarchists accused of responsibility for the massacre spread across the international wire like wild fire and was all around dramatically publicized. Seven of the eight men were convicted and sentenced to death, one of whom committed suicide in prison by exploding half his face off with a smuggled stick of dynamite, agonizing in his cell for six hours before his imminent death. The eighth defendant was given a 15-year sentence, and two of the seven were later given life sentences after an appeal to the Supreme Court. Five men, labeled 'bloody monsters,' 'cowards', 'dynamarchists' and a long list of hateful slurs, were executed by hanging, suffering a long and painful suffocation, having not broken their necks in the gallows, finally traumatizing the once-vengeful, now merciful spectators.

The executed men were immediately labeled martyrs. The entire trial willingly rested on the premise that the defendants indeed did not throw the bomb themselves but simply that they had not deterred the bomb-thrower, whoever it might have been.

Over one hundred years later, the location was designated a Chicago Landmark, and a memorial was placed in the nearby cemetery which itself was designated a National Historic Landmark, the first of its kind. The executed men became symbols of the defense of justice, linked for all eternity with the establishment of the single most important gesture in the United States for workers' rights through the dramatic yet humble shift toward a more civilized work environment. They are celebrated throughout the world, with Labor Day, International Workers' Day and any other 'workers' holiday' being set on the first of May to commemorate those unjustly executed after the Haymarket Massacre.

The desire for a day of celebration in honor of workers and their rights did not begin with the Haymarket Massacre, although the massacre very acutely altered the manner in which such a celebration would take place worldwide. Beyond its association with workers' affairs, May Day has further significance for the seasons and the structure of the calendar. A pre-Christian holiday by origin, it marks the end of the unfarmable winter in the northern hemisphere—not of winter itself, but its halfway point—and is linked through opposition to November 1, being exactly half a year away, and thus marks the opposing holiday, notable for the reaping of the harvest and the coming of the harsh winter—another midway point, called cross-quarter days, falling halfway between the solstice and equinox.

May Day was formerly the start of summer, with its

ritualistic celebration beginning the preceding night, *St. Walpurgis Abend* or *Walpurgisnacht*—hence its consideration as the opposing celebration to Halloween, precisely six months later on October 31. *Walpurgisnacht*, as Goethe has shown us in the imaginary, is characterized by fantastic and often riotous celebrations, and which, outside the literary realm, involve various traditions like the construction and adornment of the May pole with ribbons, flowers and icons.

More than ever now, *Walpurgisnacht* evokes a darkly dreamy image in my own mind. Some time ago, about a year, I encountered a dream image more dark and uncanny than I feel fully able to express. I remember my dreams without trying, they forcing themselves upon me like messages from elsewhere. My feeling is that I don't produce them but that they are revealed to me, something for me to decode. I am haunted in waking life, wondering or worrying if I've misunderstood or ignored something crucial, some information I am meant to use to affect the world, to keep something or some one or myself from harm, but usually I am too late. The vision comes and goes, not without grief or wonder, but its waking correspondent also comes and goes without my affectation. Sometimes I learn later on what I think I knew beforehand, and excitedly try to tell someone about it, about how I knew beforehand. It's always a knowing-before in a telling-after. The listener is usually embarrassed for me. My torment continues as I try to forget about it until it happens again, sometimes with the next coming night.

Black Elk proclaimed wisdom in dreams unfound in waking life, himself living a life that encompassed vastly diverging spiritual systems. After his wife's death, he took her Catholic religion, becoming a catechist while also remaining a spiritual leader of the Wakan Tanka. Perhaps a kind of harmony exists in this exceptional act of spiritual and religious integration, but it also reflects the suppression of the Sioux by the European-Americans, such that Black Elk made his conversion in light of the exhaustion and suffering of his people after the destruction at Wounded Knee. After being condemned and denounced by a Catholic priest as he looked over an ailing boy, Black Elk himself began to question the solidity of his native healing powers, or perhaps of his approach to healing, and humbly and graciously joined the white man's religion. Yet, without a doubt, such a transition was necessarily infused with Black Elk's deep and ancient spiritual presence given to him through the world of the Six Grandfathers and his childhood calling as a *wichasha wakan*, like his father and grandfather before him. Black Elk's pure devotion to the multiplicity of spiritual ways cannot be reduced merely to happenstance. His interest in the possibility of the Great Spirit entering the world through duplicity began long before the pain and carnage at Wounded Knee. Healing came to Black Elk in many forms, many that he himself could not understand but that would anchor him in their paths.

I take courage from Black Elk, and as his story floats through my head, my current thoughts are strangely bound to that exceptionally darkly dreamy image I had encountered during my last night sleeping on the outskirts in the countryside of *Ulaanbaatar*. I was in Mongolia exactly one year ago. There were orphan children, and I went because I was an orphan child too, not in the same way as them, but I was compelled, and so I went and so I helped them and they helped me.

I have recently been having strange dreams of my mom, and not, I believe, because she is gone now (this time forever) but because I feel something has been compelling her presence toward me. Since my trip to Mongolia I have been invaded by her appearance more than ever. In one she is wearing new glasses out of which she cannot see. In another she is a child speaking about her beloved gramps to no one. (Or am I there too, her audience?) In another we are together, my mother again just a child, overlooking her own poor mother as she struggled and died in childbirth, the baby along with her. In another she is instructing me in proper swimming form with consternation and a severe, stone-cut expression. There are too many to keep count. There are too many to reflect upon. We never had swimming lessons. We never had any kind of lessons. We were often left dirty and hungry, in the dark and cold for days on end. We played hobo and survival and indoor camping. We ate marshmallows cooked in the fireplace for breakfast and stale croutons for dinner in the dark because we had no electricity, because those are the only things we could find in the house, scavenging high and low for food in all the cupboards with no adults to help. We bought one-cent pieces of candy shaped like strawberries at the gas station. Across those thousands of days, she was there and not there for thousands more until she is now never there again.

The details of the darkly dreamy image in my mind today from that night in *Ulaanbaatar* were not of my mom. They are once again deeply vivid and have developed into a narrative. The story is so peculiar I'm unable to shake it. I recall here the details: two young girls were sent through time to make things right that might have happened somehow wrongly deep in the past. And so they arrived somewhere, casual, in their jeans, out of place but calm, knowing. They found a woman having a baby in a telephone booth. The explanation I was given, that fell into my head without its being spoken, was that the child was named after one of the girls, along with a German diminutive suffix, so the baby's name was *Heinlein*.

The two girls immediately traveled to the mid-17th Century and saw a strangely clothed man, whose face they could not at first see. He was holding a leather satchel, had a pocket watch, dark hair and a beard. He gave them a fantastically styled key, holding it out to them on a short black string, and it was understood that this key was the token of engagement that he should have given to the woman who had just bore the child in another time and who, in fact, maybe had been one of the two girls themselves. He urged them to return 42 years in the past to stop a certain coming marriage signified by the key.

I found myself 42 years in the future still to be un-married, the man with the watch explained to me.

For that reason, he continued to explain in his own words, I sought to return to the past to find this woman and to marry her. He paused and added, Somehow later I felt the idea to be a tremendous mistake.

He could not yet fathom the consequences. It seemed that he had disrupted things as they were to be, as they should be, and in his estimation, it was up to these two girls to correct this misdeed, as they walked, walking across old, dark railroad tracks, calmly, silently, suspended in a space that does not actually exist or that no longer exists. They didn't believe why this desire was something to be corrected, since it seemed as though what he did, what had happened with the man and the key and the woman in the booth with the child, that it was all for what it should be, and nothing should be undone. Nothing could be undone.

I was left wondering if he had married or not, or if in doubting the marriage, in the presence of Heinlein to the girls, the man with the watch had eliminated the event itself, as though time was not being undone but re-aligned; as though nothing had changed but that even the correction itself was already part of what time held, to our appearances, inevitably. The key was still in the man's possession, as he passed it on to the two girls, and the bride he had sought was neither with him nor strangely, as he passed the key, did it seem that she had ever been. Where she existed was unknown to me, unknown to him; but the child was born in the booth,

and all through the events connected to this still unknown child, I knew that the man with the watch felt
a deep fear, perhaps a fear of the child itself as though
its existence brought to his own a weariness, delivering
a message of fearful apprehension. Through it, through
the power of the birth of Heinlein, the man with the
watch felt this fear and apprehension in himself that
gave him reason to question, or even remember, his desire to alter or attempt to re-alter what one should be
wary of altering once it is past.

2.

I awoke that day feeling, as I always do, as though I'm being ripped out of a reality with a force that makes me confused and lost for some time as I lie there in bed. I was exhausted, displaced, conflicted and aware that I was meant to be participating in a world that was completely different from the one in which I had just found myself. Not only that, but the waking world felt for a time less real and like a grand imposition on the project or agenda in which I was a part of in the dream world. I forced myself to let go of those obligations and feelings, that intense effort to exist, and to understand what was happening around me in that other world. The sensation of transitioning from the intensity of its realness to the letting-go of its force and acknowledging its unrealness was overwhelming and debilitating. What seemed to be crucial tasks became figments of the meaningless unconscious. I bridged two worlds, quickly recognizing the flatness of the one and the nonexistence of the other. I was lost, disappointed, confused, aching to return and yet relieved to let go of the task that had no logic and behaved as though the world's balance hinged on apprehending its meaning accurately.

Black Elk's inclination toward such vast openness, uniting dreams and reality, led him to become part of many differing traditions as a result of the uncommon circumstances in his life. Nor was his fusion with the white man's culture limited to his spiritual forms. I wonder if maybe the message from my visions is how my fate too may be connected to the joining of bodies of thought, converging everything seen and heard into one big cosmic understanding. And then what? I asked myself. It's frightening to think that there is something I am supposed to do with it, or even that there is something I'm supposed to do, or even that I would think that I would believe that these darkly dreamy images are giving me something to do and to be and also to share.

As was the case with many prominent Native American figures at the time, Black Elk briefly toured the country in 1887 with Buffalo Bill's Wild West, as an extraordinary spectacle, like the other proud, traditionally-clad representatives of unknown world cultures. As may be expected, Black Elk found the experience disappointing. We try to take into account several factors when considering how this sideshow circus was constructed.

The son of anti-slavery Quakers, William 'Buffalo Bill' Cody spent his early years living a variety of lives including Buffalo hunter, goldrusher, soldier, Pony Express rider and finally a showman when in 1872 he traveled to Chicago and formed a performance troupe lasting ten years. The show toured the U. S. and Europe and included well-known military personnel, Native Americans and the peoples of various horse-riding cultures including Turks, Mongols, Arabs and Georgians, each showcasing their finery in costume and performance. One of Buffalo Bill's best-known performers was the sharp shooter Annie Oakley. In 1883 Buffalo

Bill's Wild West was born, to become in 1893 Buffalo Bill's Wild West and Congress of Rough Riders of the World.

Vice President Roosevelt adopted the moniker 'Rough Riders' for the first volunteer cavalry of the United States, those asked to fight the Spanish-American War, the Army having been weakened too severely by the Civil War thirty years prior. As homage not just to Buffalo Bill's tough man circus, Roosevelt's Rough Riders seems to be a direct nod to Annie Oakley, promoter of women in combat. She had already written to President McKinley of her personal interest in supporting the Spanish-American War through an addition of 50 'lady sharpshooters' – the offer rejected but still influenced Roosevelt's later adoption of the name of his volunteer sharp shooting soldiers.

Woman or not, Oakley was confident and unsurpassed. We ask ourselves how her skill was founded and how she knew she was capable or worthy or interested in entering a male-dominated field. She was beautiful and strong – qualities we strangely isolate and admire in women, but the accounts of her life are necessarily exaggerated in whatever form, so that she was either some ideal representation of the sophisticated beauty in a man's world, or the underdog hotshot treated less than her worth. We can mark the time in its entirety as something incorrect, and pride ourselves on what has changed for the better though we ourselves are not responsible and though it was figures like Oakley herself who changed it as they lived out their own real lives and hardships.

We are conscious of our desires, we are owners of our own desires because Oakley herself had entered the world and lived a life that could show us what might be possible. Oakley gave herself to us, and so I have to wonder, as we all wonder, what it is for me to give as well.

We seem to be astounded at the possibility of Oakley in her time and place, but we fail to understand that all of what has passed has been that which has made our thoughts of surprise and delight possible at all. Oakley is inside us to the extent that she extended to us the possibility both to question and change inequality but also to remember it already as something horrific in all its forms. And yet Oakley herself was herself when she was, when she was herself, and this is what we fail to see. To continue to fail to see that is to continue to enact what we think is its very failure. It is not surprising that Oakley was well-respected, was accepted, was able to break shooting records against men and against other sharpshooting women and to hold meetings with heads of state around the world. Why is this surprising to us? It was not unordinary because it simply was, it was Annie Oakley, she in her way.

Oakley died at sixty-six from a fatal form of anemia. She had been married to her first competitor, Frank E. Butler, who in 1882 lost a significant shoot-out bet, then courted and married his opponent. In his despair over the loss of his wife after over 45 years together, Butler stopped eating and died eighteen days later.

Oakley once met with Kaiser Wilhelm II, maybe it

was in 1889, shooting the ashes off his cigarette, much to the demise of later historians who had wished her shot failed her, offering a change in the course of history that would have eliminated the Kaiser as the source of World War I. A myth to be spun, an eternal regret, an absurd and shameless request in hindsight. After the outbreak of the war, Oakley sent the Austrian emperor a letter asking for a chance at a second shot. A letter left unanswered.

Kaiser Wilhelm II probably never imagined his eternal reputation as a scoundrel. He may likely have thought instead he was choosing a life of military and political fame, success, victory – all the accoutrement to go with the monarch. Naïve, bombastic, impish behavior that colors a critique he could not have imagined. Curious how we imagine ourselves in life and how we are unable to imagine ourselves in death but also unable to imagine that being something other than what we are to ourselves. What we do in life is based on some ethereal sense of our individual existences as universally and eternally meaningful. Our concepts of space and time guide us to perform acts that have meaning in their performance but, more importantly, in the greater weight given to their existence as performances that exist outside of the moment of their being acted. We are separated from our actions immediately, and they take on lives that move spatially and temporally beyond our own. We are aware of this, if only ever so slightly. It might be hidden to our conscious minds entirely, but it is an unseen force that affects the ways in which the billions of us give meaning to the world.

Kaiser Wilhelm II was the last Kaiser of Germany and King of Prussia. Arrogant, short tempered, he was a poor statesman and strategist, and, as a primary ally of Austria-Hungary's war on the Kingdom of Serbia that began the insurmountable destruction of the Great War in 1914, Wilhelm II was forced into exile in 1918, with the absolute defeat of the Central Powers and the dismantling entirely of both the legendary Austro-Hungarian and Ottoman Empires.

Austria-Hungary had the desire to weaken and even annihilate Serbia altogether, and so when the young Gavrilo Princip took advantage of his second chance to assassinate the visiting Archduke Franz Ferdinand in his motorcade through Sarajevo, the resulting conflict between the two nations ultimately led to World War I. On the pretext of 'civilization', brought forth in this instance by Austria-Hungary, imperialism continued to stretch its shadowy heavy hand across the full European continent and far beyond around the world. Nations bound to the empire by treaties, as was Russia, were forced to swear allegiance during the oncoming assaults and enter the war by paradoxical force of gratitude.

It began with a request by Emperor Franz Joseph of Austria-Hungary to Archduke Franz Ferdinand, heir to the Austro-Hungarian throne, to travel to Bosnia with his wife Sophie in the summer of 1914 to preside over military maneuvers taking place in Sarajevo. As they left the display, their caravan was bombed by a roadside terrorist, instigated by the first of four amateurs located along the royal couple's path, acting out his part in the attack, throwing a handmade bomb followed swiftly by swallowing a cyanide tablet, that ultimately proved faulty, and jumping in the river. The bomb itself was deflected and instead blew up the military car that was following up the royal pair's convoy. The assailant was dragged from the river, which, it is told, was only inches deep. He was found vomiting, not dying, from his tablet and was there arrested. Only 19 years old, he was sentenced to 20 years in prison; averting execution unlike the other detained conspirators, and instead dying behind those same bars nevertheless a short two years later in 1916 from consumption. During the trial, the youth expressed regret and was said to have been pardoned by the royal children.

In a strange turn of events that created that fateful day, the royal couple ultimately decided to ride directly to the hospital to visit the wounded from the military convoy of the earlier assassination attempt. It is said that their driver, unaware of the new route planned, took a false path through the city that put them back in an accidental confrontation with one of the attempted assassins whose initial will had weakened during his first opportunity as the motorcade passed, leaving him paralyzed and unable to throw his bomb. Yet, here, now, as the car halted, reversed and attempted to right itself onto the correct path, 19-year-old Princip walked up to the paused vehicle and fired two shots into the open convertible from a distance of five feet. The first shot hit the Archduke in the neck. As the blood spurted violently from his mouth, his startled wife bluntly implored him to tell her what on earth had just befallen him. In that very moment, however, as she simultaneously leaned toward him, all in an instant, her abdomen was penetrated by the second bullet, and she immediately slumped over upon her husband where she quickly died. Gazing down upon her, holding her in his arms, historians report that the Archduke begged her, with voice raised and loving, to live for their children, not knowing that he himself had but minutes to his own life. Indeed, his panicked driver asked him of his wound to which he replied, in a voice becoming ever-more faint: *Es ist nichts. Es ist nichts.* It is nothing.

Austria-Hungary's response to this act of terrorism was to necessitate a declaration of war against Serbia, as the kingdom was unable and unwilling to meet the extreme demands of recompense ordered by the still-expanding Germanic empire. The Central Powers, which included the German and Ottoman Empires and the Kingdom of Bulgaria, suffered great losses by joining with Austria-Hungary in the sixth bloodiest war of all time. Kaiser Wilhelm lived out the rest of his life in exile in the Netherlands.

I consider that how this story is remembered is not much thought to be a question of accuracy. It seems there is a time and a place for accuracy, or what we call accuracy is malleable, depending on the circumstances of the story or, as they say, who the storyteller may be. That the Archduke spoke the words he did of his love for his wife and family and of his honor and his overcoming of the pain in his final breath, that his wife died immediately and did not suffer, that she died upon him in a gesture directly motivated by her care for him, that the first would-be assassin was humiliatingly dragged from four inches of river water with a failed suicide tablet in his gut, that the assassin himself acted twice cowardly – these items alert the reader not to inaccuracies necessarily but supremely to the arbitrarity not of writing history but of remembering it. It is evident that the recording of history takes the point of view of the greatest in power or at least the most influential in some significant regard, in the specific capacity necessary. It is, however, the remembering of history that infiltrates most deeply, widely through the base of knowledge, through the roots so that history will be known not as the forceful imposition of the storyteller but legitimately as a conglomerate effort at the piecing together of elements. It is certain that the reader understands how events are recreated through perspectival forces, yet how they are deliberately misrepresented can never be known.

We forgive the historians as they undertake the honorable effort of melding together all of the archeological navigations that lead to the collective woven text that moves across ages.

3.

Some time ago I had been in Spitalfields market thinking about history-making, story-making. I had walked through the bazaar after a particularly lengthy run through the city of London. It was already a while ago, just after returning from Mongolia and before leaving again for Paris. I arrived in dusty and salt-encrusted running clothes, moving in the crowded neighborhood on a Sunday afternoon with the splay of the weekly flea market. Surrounded by the stalls, perfumes and wares, I started to feel myself reconnected to the story of the man with the watch. It wasn't in the memory of the market where I found his tale again, but in what came after the market, yet the recollection of the entire experience at the market even now continues to evoke a new tension in me so that each detail of the passing days grows louder, more palpable, paradoxically separating and blurring reality and dream. As time stretches out now across the past year and I walk again in memory through Spitalfields, I can feel something changing in me, something impending, living, an awareness, a history and a connection, reliving both these memories and the darkly dreamy images, feeling them colliding.

The market itself is always infinitely lively. There at its unmarked threshold, as I passed through the narrow outdoor corridors, I observed how different corners of the tightly packed area housed different groups of people, which between themselves sold similar wares, similar foods, of similar ethnicities. In one area I'd find the north Africans, in another the southeast Asians, in another the punks, the posh and prim, the hippies and hipsters, the youth, the blacks, the whites, the tans and pinks and rainbows, the greens and the browns. The shops put tables in the road, wide enough only for massive, moving groups of people, a car advancing slower than the kids pushing each other along both its sides. The makeshift street restaurants sold readymade juices and sandwiches, cooking hot, pungent lunches over giant grills made from barrels, charring meat, chicken masala bright red, curried rice bright yellow, blackened corn and gritty, dark potatoes, endless mixed aromas floating in the air, conga drums, reggae, house, funk, electro, folk colliding, dancing, jerking, smiling, swinging spatulas, purses, babies.

Like at the flea markets of Paris, the non-licensed marketers around the corners would bring out their junk on blankets on towels on tables in tents in vans on bikes. A young Chinese youth saw me interested in his WWI and II goggles and gave me the history on a rare Russian pair, the leather dried and broken, the goggles so small like the Napoleonic armor in museums in Vienna and Paris and Berlin. Fit for a child. I suddenly imagined a cartoon in action of a boy, or perhaps Snoopy, flying with his Russian aviator goggles wearing a suit of armor. The red baron.

The images in school and late evening history programs of the gas masks from WWI, they always looked cryptic and skeletal. They are emblems of death, after and not before the fact. Such design is meant to flatter life, the shape of the face, the eyes, the expression of the eyes, the delicate structure of the face and how it needs air, sight, freedom of movement. We forgive those historians again or ourselves in this instance, in all of our collective impressions and memories of violence that supersede questions of design of forethought of purpose without a clear face. Instead all we can do now is identify them with the horrors that those behind committed or of the atrocities received.

Perhaps sitting in his kitchen one day, setting his bike down on the gravel path earlier to run off and help his mom cooking a stew, an old school boy engineer,

I see, the old school boy engineer grabbed his corner-worn notepad from the table and drew two perfect circles side by side.

This is what we need, he excitedly thought and went on to construct something first to be used in the mines and later developed during war.

But the gas mask would remain uncomfortable and stifling with awkward fitting parts, hard and stiff against the soft flesh of the face, eyes squinting through blurry, scratched, dew-dropped lenses, jaws and teeth aching biting down on the mouthpiece, the chemical taste rolling over the tongue against the cheeks, reminiscent of Kafka's description of the literary execution device from *In der Strafkolonie*. Strapped to a literal deathbed in the center of a huge medieval apparatus, the prisoner's body turns and turns across a field of hundreds of delicate needles that tear into his flesh, writing his crime and punishment with each intricate vibration, the precision of the turning of the cogs, the design of the mechanism to wash away blood and vomit, finally casting off the body into a death pit as it becomes an enlightened corpse.

What we see of the gasmask: a ghostly image of a frozen soldier, brown and grey and dirty and faded altogether, nothing gazing out from the giant holes that now look more like the sockets of skeletons, death looming. Of course death looming. Something about this looming initiated a tangible yet remote presence of the story of the man with the watch, as I remembered the market.

This gas mask would be used to protect the frozen solider from the death he's causing or is being caused around him. We might envision an image we've seen in a forgotten documentary of a Vietnamese couple hiding with their children and the bodies of three others in a cave the size of a closet. They found two dead soldiers after the hard rain in November; those silently borrowed gas masks the sole reason three survived until the end of the war that coming spring. Sitting motionless, melding into the earth that did not give them up, not proud, not grateful, no thoughts or expressions but alive.

I put down the Russian goggles. I'm unable to spend £12 on anything, and I only wanted them for a show that evening with a costume theme. I found a pair of bug-eye shaped sunglasses across the way for £4 and bought those instead.

That night we went to a burlesque circus performance in a small theatre. Their theme was bugs, and the performers were dressed like insects. They climbed ropes and twirled, they battled and hissed, they tap-danced, they contorted. The audience too was dressed in costume. We were insects. I was a butterfly. During the show I was thinking of the woman giving birth in the telephone booth, and I wondered what happened to her child and if I would learn its fate. The experience from the afternoon lingered but was not oppressive.

Two children in the row in front of me were dressed as heroes and were swinging batons at the performers who descended upon them. They were laughing.

The show risked becoming a game instead of a performance. The amusement that the children displayed was not from the show but from their interaction with it, and yet they wanted to join it by destroying it, to remove it from the stage and thrust it into the ordinary of their own game of battle dress-up. I think later that this might be inborn Brechtian behavior. We held our breath for the fallout, but the boys were loyal, or their parents were loyal, and they did not go too far. The performers returned to the stage. The children caught their breath, and the audience sighed and smiled with its neighbors. The boys were excited yet depleted, flustered, vibrating, not quite ready to end the disruption that their joining caused. They were like Bedouin warriors crossing the desert on camels, fearsome, fearless, tireless. They were loyal to themselves, but, more importantly, still trustworthy to the empire.

It is true that the form of the Bedouins is fearsome to an outsider, and their loyalties run deep, and yet the closer the connection to one form of clansman, the deeper the potential division to another. *I against my brother, my brothers and I against my cousins, then my cousins and I against strangers.* We might say that any empire is composed of a collection of banned warriors who are otherwise one another's enemies. I don't know if Buffalo Bill had Bedouins, but I am certain of his individual power to manifest that union in his commercial empire, or I might ask what kind of unity did his empire have? In the open desert of the Arabian peninsula, each Bedouin is a warrior unto himself and by step in unison with each other apart from him. The Bedouins collectively are united at a remote, chain-linked distance to the Arabian empire.

I thought of those warriors as I recalled the Chinese boy with the Russian goggles and his old map of central Asia lain out on the rug, transporting me back to recent memories of looking over the plateaus of inner Mongolia, hearing the calls and laughter of orphan children as I worked alongside them on their crude farm. There in the dust, I could see nothing but hills and long stretches of barren land circling me in every direction. Dry animal bones lying around as though carelessly scattered, wild horses running across the brush, an occasional dog drinking from a low stream miles away, barely visible. We lived in yurts and spent our time building a well with sand taken from a small stretch near the outhouse then mixed with limestone brought in from *Ulaanbaatar*. The cement had to be carefully sifted before it could be mixed, poured and spackled across rough stones and stacked around the hole for the well. The work was hard, the days long. We awoke to instant coffee and harsh, sandy black tea that had an aftertaste of mutton, softened with condensed milk and served with thick, biscuit-style cookies given exceptional longevity through preservatives.

We worked in the fields from sunrise until shortly before noon when it became too hot. The children showed us how to delicately pull weeds without ruining the small, growing potatoes among them. Lunch was last night's leftovers followed by the chalky cookies and more coffee. Meals had sparse fresh ingredients: potatoes and onions with an overabundance of mayonnaise; there were canned peas and tomatoes, anything that would last the perpetual famine. Once a week there were fresh tomatoes and cucumbers if the truck arrived from town. We worked on the well in the afternoon. Dinner was a great welcome. After more cookies and coffee, we sang, played games, walked, rested. I ran up the plateaus, crunching bones, dead grass, slate underfoot. A crude rod supported by rocks erected at the top like an unadorned maypole faced north with the skull of a beast nearby. Horses ran below. A wolf searched for water in the dry brush in the valley. I laid down each night with a view of the Mongolian sky and its wide-open darkness bordered by the even darker mountains.

The yurts were enclosed by a small, broken fence, and beyond the fence were the hills, plateaus, and more distant yurts of nomads, the free horses, the bones and the enormously deep underground storage pits for the potatoes. The children filled the pits at the end of the summer. The surplus kept them fed throughout the year.

The sun set on the Mongolian landscape like a strong but fleshy hand coming down upon the soft down on the head of a chick. It was the force of the shift from day to night, both cumbersome like an unwanted gesture of direction and soothing like the feel of a cool, wet cloth on a fevered brow. The stars loomed large, bright, overwhelming, peaceful, mysterious, lighting up the silhouette of the mountains on the horizon.

The description of the map through the Chinese boy's words were absorbed by my own images of Mongolia, coming before my imagination again later that night in the theatre, and I could imagine the scene with its physical outline in the center of the world. There is a vast space both infinitely unrecognizable and yet so close to the heart as to be frightening: I realized at that moment that the beaten, old map of the Chinese boy with the Russian military goggles was dated 1650, the same year that the man with the watch considered his mistake and encountered the two girls, giving them the key.

Sitting in the theatre, I matched that view of Mongolia with my new view of the Chinese boy's ancient map, while watching the insect circus and wondering if the man with the watch could know of his sacrifice or of his risk. I thought about my decision to work with the orphans in Mongolia, the darkly image at the end of my stay and the now unraveling story before me and how perhaps they were somehow all linked to the equally perplexing dreams of my mother.

It was there in the theatre with the bug burlesque circus that I realized the man with the watch could not know but would only be able to believe in knowing. It happened so long ago, I was confused as to how the events could still be unfolding before me in this way, as though the Bedouins were still crossing the vast plains of the Gobi or flying west toward the Arabic edges of the Ottoman Empire.

In the same year that Dr. Johnson defined, for centuries to come, the qualities of 17th century metaphysical poetry, the Ottoman Empire was itself, like John Donne's England, in a state of reformation. In the late 1590s Donne introduced the world to his use of wit, metaphor, imagery through an eccentric catachresis. It was this form that Dr. Johnson condescendingly called metaphysical poetry, for it was overburdened by erudition and lacking in sentiment. T. S. Eliot revitalized the form in the early 20th Century, reclaiming instead the unity of sensibility set down by the metaphysicals, declaring theirs a most complete form of poetry: such a combination of erudition and sense. While Eliot left Unitarianism to join the Anglican Church, Donne reformed 350 years earlier from Catholicism, humbly believing not in a conversion but in the natural succession of the shift fueled by his personal, spiritual commitment.

The metaphysicals saw poetry as a vehicle for transmitting clarity of emotion and sensibility alongside articulated historical knowledge. Not just the clearest thoughts should benefit from the best use of the body of past histories but the clearest feelings, sentiments and expressions of the delicate body. To conjoin the two—thought and feeling—in the structure of a poem further involved both dexterity and depth of skill, of language and of learning. Venturing into the unknown with the supplies of the known, the metaphysicals paradoxically risked tradition to explore its application in a present moment full of conflated images, far-fetched metaphors, plays in words. Metaphysical poetry could itself be seen as a reformation akin to Donne's own: moving from the forms of antiquity, made stale through convention and abuse, toward a newness of spirit that would nevertheless still retain a firmly held purpose, a core of value that itself could motivate that very change.

A handful of years later in 1798, after Dr. Johnson's essay, when the Ottoman Empire defeated the invading Napoleon, the explorer Joseph Walker was born in Tennessee; first white man to see Yosemite Valley. In his middle 30s Walker set out west in search of a usable land route to California. The path he forged was occupied by anxious gold diggers several decades later, but it was his own acutely sensory experience on that trip of the first sight of the Yosemite Valley for which he is now remembered. We can try to recall Walker entering the valley and what awe must have fallen into his eye and down his throat into his bowels and back out through the puff of exhaled breath that met the late afternoon sun across the granite monoliths around him. We project on it too much knowledge of the space between his life and ours. We envy him this encounter without recognizing how the reimagining and retelling of the tale cannot contain the more accurate variety of experiences affecting him as a human being in that repeated instant of the perpetual unexpected. We instill the vision with the heroic, as though the heroic itself could be embodied in any experience and not simply exist as the result of a storytelling or of a recording of events after they have impacted the political landscape.

4.

Remembering the theatre with the burlesque insect circus, I wandered in my mind once again across the market earlier that same day and again the Chinese boy's map from frayed and dirtied edges toward the center and back, and thinking of that map at Spital-fields, I tried to remember the borders along the edges of an elongated Mongolia and wondered for example how far did Russia reach and what shapes had filled the spaces in the west, now Kazakhstan and other former Soviet republics. I seemed to be aware that somewhere in the history of the man with the watch is the story of his ancestors from Prussia.

I was trying to link the Chinese boy's map over and over with my time in Mongolia, wanting the mental images to come into motion on their own, to reveal their progression to me to give me new information so I could connect them, decode their message, like a celluloid turning from one wheel of the projector to the other, revealing a single, smooth track of images that move so quickly as to deceive the eye, washing it with bright white light, blurring the black edges of the film strip. If I could recall the events that led up to the darkly dream image and somehow project them on to the Chinese boy's map, could I not figure out what was coming to pass? What I might be seeing or have seen? What I could learn or understand or at least extract? I must try. I always must try.

In remembering the map lain out on the ground in

Spitalfields market and re-imagining my Mongolian experiences, I held firm that it would be there in that old outline of Prussia that the man with the watch would be able to trace back his encounter with this new Hein figure. As I sat there still, thinking too of the spectacle of the insect circus, I thought of my own heritage going back to the same lost geography of Prussia and tried to imagine where the ties crossed leading the man with the watch to look for Hein or encounter the girls and what it might mean to recover what, to him, had happened by mistake.

It seems paradoxical to speak of recent Prussian history, and yet it has not been gone 100 years. Prussian by birth, Friedrich Nietzsche was born in Röcken in 1844, eventually renouncing his national citizenship upon taking up teaching duties in Switzerland. Unable to become a Swiss citizen, however, he remained stateless for the rest of his life dying in 1900, despite his native land itself not ceasing to exist until 1947.

More than any other perhaps, a thick vein of Goethe runs through Nietzsche's work, with many critics believing Goethe could have been Nietzsche's personal vision of his Übermensch. Goethe, like Nietzsche, highly valorized solitude, humanity and art, but also invoked the theory of the necessity of contempt, misapprehension and other marginally appreciated ideas, through the significance of their given valuation and potential revaluation in society. Crossing fields both literary and scientific, it was surely Goethe who also compelled Nietzsche to develop a broad style in his own body of writing. Nietzsche gave his hand to music; Goethe to painting. As a rare figure of unsurpassable singularity, Goethe lent his work a diversity that encompasses an even greater range of subjects from his widely regarded and universal color theory to his philosophical fairy-tales.

Goethe's *Märchen* of the snake and the lily is an allegorical and highly stylized rendering of Schiller's theory on the attainment of freedom by the soul and the promise of aesthetic and personal growth through the union of the sensible and supersensible (physical life harmonized with the actualization of the inner self), as found in his 1794 study, *Über die ästhetische Erziehung des Menschen* (*On the Aesthetic Education of Men*), inspired by the corrupted, over-rational philosophy of the French Revolution. Goethe's fairytale tells the intricate story of the love between a prince and a lily, mediated through elaborate details of a complex series of events that begin one late evening on the side of a river.

I had not read the *Märchen* until after I heard the story of the man with the watch. I had not read the *Märchen* until after Mongolia but before the map and the Chinese boy and the insect circus. It has many intricate parts, and despite having an outcome to share, the individual elements are enormously sententious, though the reader often cannot decipher why.

Two excited will-o-the-wisps appear, engaging a weary ferryman to cross them upon restless waters, their frenetic and flighty behavior nearly capsizing the boat throughout the journey. As recompense to the upset driver, the two wisps shake their lithe bodies, showering the bottom of the vessel with many fine gold pieces. Shocked and anxious, the ferryman angrily and swiftly refuses their payment scolding them for nearly flooding the entire river, explaining the water itself cannot tolerate such metal making any contact with it. As the fragile wisps mindlessly attempt to slip away, the ferryman retains them forcefully and demands they bring him instead three cabbages, three artichokes and three large onions. In their discomfort, they agree and flee, and the ferryman swiftly rows away, far away, until he reaches beyond the waters and up toward high and barren rocks, among which he throws the dangerous gold pieces.

The noise of the falling gold awakens a snake below who greedily eats the pieces, and finds its body quickly becoming phosphorescent. Extremely pleased with this transformation, the snake seeks out the mysterious benefactor, eventually finding the wisps themselves, who continue to provide a seemingly endless supply of gold to the insatiable snake. As gratitude the snake offers the wisps its servitude, to which they respond with a request to find their worship, the lily. A difficult demand, replies the snake, as the lily is across the restless river, which can no longer be traversed by means of the ferryman, as he may not transport any back whom he's already transported hence, and so the wisps must go either on the back of the snake at piercing midday, which they are wont to refuse in their fragility, or in the powerful shadow of the otherwise powerless giant.

Leaving them to decide, the snake returns to the rocks with great excitement in hopes of illuminating the many subterranean objects, which it has only heretofore felt by entwining its body around in the darkness. The snake finds the first of four kings who asks:

How did you arrive?

Through the cleft.

What is more noble than gold?

Light.

And more vivid than light?

Speech.

The snake meets the three other kings, each being of a different metal composition, but first an old man whose light illuminates only when in the presence of another illumination. Before the old man is able to share the fourth and most precious of secrets to the kings, which he has just learned from the snake, he and the snake vanish through the rock, with the light of the old man converting all the stone it touches into gold.

Returning to his hut, the old man finds his wife in despair over an unwelcome visitation by the wisps who have extracted all the gold from the hut, filled their lean bodies and proceeded to shake out gold pieces onto the floor. The old woman explains how their dog Mops ate the transformed metal, causing him a sudden death.

The old man sends his heartbroken wife out with the corpse of old Mops, which has become an onyx, to seek help from the beautiful lily and also to confer the three cabbages, three artichokes and three large onions to the ferryman on behalf of the wisps. As the old woman

approaches the river, however, the shadow of the powerless giant steals one each of her cabbages, artichokes
and onions, leaving the unsympathetic ferryman an-
gered at the reduced payment, forcing the old woman
to plunge her sweet hand into the river, blackening and
shrinking it, and with that gesture making a promise to
the waters that she will return before next day with the
missing vegetables. On her way to the beautiful lily, the
old woman meets the prince, and as they walk together
they discover a passage over the river via a bridge that
has been created by the arched back of the snake, who,
after their crossing, accompanies them.

The travelers find the lily mourning the loss of her
canary. She restores life to Mops, adopting him as her
own and giving the canary to the old woman to transform into a topaz, but in that instant the prince rushes
toward the lily in desperation for her embrace and is
instantly killed. The prince and canary lie together in
a circle created by the snake who holds its own tail in
its mouth.

The tale here becomes vastly complex with events
that have hardly any logical bearing upon any others.
The prince's life is tenderly restored, as the snake is simultaneously turned into a variety of gems and eventually into a grand bridge for thousands to cross. The
old man instructs the old woman to bathe in the river,
restoring her body. The wisps consume the gold from
the fourth king, after which he crumbles into ruins.
The temple in which the kings reside moves like a ship
toward the river, crushing the old hut of the ferryman,
turning it into a temple.

The three kings emerge and announce the three constituents that have sway upon the earth: wisdom, appearance and power, to which the prince adds the fourth: the power of love, but the old man modifies the claim, declaring: *Love does not rule, but directs, and that is better.* The giant's shadow is rendered powerless, the old man and woman become young lovers again, and the wisps disperse the gold from the fourth and destroyed king over the peoples crossing the river, who fight and injure one another to collect the unexpected treasure. When the gold ceases falling, each goes about another task, and the tale concludes with the declaration that the kings' temple still remains the most visited on earth.

The snake is Schiller's bridge between one's reality and one's ideal inner self. How does the human soul become whole and free? Not through external forces but from within. The prince undertakes a transformation by marrying the supernatural lily. As each soul finds itself in external expression, a community is formed that collectively prizes the unified individuals' enlightenment. Yet the sacrifices necessary in Goethe are often dark and foreboding, and the behavior of the recipients equally does not convey gratitude but expectation and even indifference. No one feels sorrow or even admiration at the snake's self-sacrifice for the life of the prince. The desire of the goal, the union of the inner and outer self, often outweighs the consequences that negatively affect some other, or perhaps Goethe demonstrates the apathetic acceptance of destruction that perpetually resides within the breast of creation.

...ein einzelner hilft nicht, sondern wer sich mit vielen zur rechten Stunde vereinigt.

The implication may be not that the group succeeds where the individual fails but that individuals may be sacrificed for the betterment of the group. Nevertheless, it still remains in each individual's power to unite, to establish the community and, through it, the self, and to do so from an inner desire to actualize one's perfection of self—the manifestation of the ideal. *A single individual does not help, but the one who unites himself with many at the right hour.*

Part of being human is to wonder if this union between inner and outer self is possible. Through the haunting tales of Goethe we arrive at a picture even more confounding where relying on the imaginary to enhance the real is disrupted not only by an actual infiltration of the real by the imaginary, thus eliminating the boundary between the two, but by the painful consequences of the imaginary on the real that are often met with an apathy from us that serves to highlight, on a universal level, how paradoxically insignificant and precious the individual experience may very well be. The world is miraculously constituted as a whole with or without our unique experiences and our memories. Our imaginaries come and go. It is only if they manage to enter into the real, and at that on a grand scale, that they can take any place in remembered histories. But even then, they have become something other than what they were when they began.

Just as well, dreams come alive, and despite their elevating of the real to an ecstatic state, they also corrupt the real, tearing apart its simplicity, violating its dependability, ultimately providing access not simply to beautiful visions but also to horrors. When Faust makes his pact with Mephistopheles, it is evident, precisely as the overarching moral to the tale, that he not comprehend the devastating sacrifices his initial choice will force him soon to make. He is lost in the impending illusion of the imaginary. He is already lost in the fantastic impact it shall make on reality, and so when the poor and innocent Gretchen goes mad with despair and drowns her newborn child (their newborn child), it is with human pity, and perhaps more strongly self-pity, that Faust implores Mephistopheles to rectify her subsequent unjust imprisonment.

What shall we make of his awareness of her fate coming only on the paradoxical *Walpurgisnacht* where flying witches mock and are mocked, satanic rituals are carried out, supernatural chants are sung, orgies intoxicate the landscape, and the delicate Gretchen suddenly appears to the surprised Faust in the form of a dream image within the terrifying face of Medusa?

Goethe confounds the senses. The tragedy of Gretchen's fate is overwritten by the medieval comedy of sorcerers and witches taking place. The innocent but fallen Gretchen is condemned to death on her wedding day. She is a sacrifice. The court is indifferent. Moreover, in his own moment of truth, Faust does not submit himself to the holy justice of accepting the same punishment. He instead allows himself to be borne away by Mephistopheles before he can be condemned; he leaves Gretchen to her madness and to justice, and yet one suspects that his must be a far greater condemnation. Isn't it? Gretchen is saved, Goethe tells us, but nevertheless she has lost her child and her purity and her very life. Faust suffers with guilt and lives to endure that guilt. Yet, I feel, he has still achieved something far more real by linking his fate to the darkness of imagination.

The truth is disturbed by the chanting and cackling voices of the spirits crossing between the real and imaginary of *Walpurgisnacht*. A vast and permanent shadow covers Mt. Brocken where black magic is performed and Faust saw the beautiful vision of Gretchen for the last time.

Faust's hell is personal, and as he leaves Gretchen to her mortal fate, she cries out to him one last time, *Heinrich! Heinrich!*

*****

Mt. Brocken has been the real home to witches since the 17th century gathering at its summit on May Day, *Walpurgisnacht*, in the attempt to actualize the imaginary tales of such events as recorded in earlier medieval literature. How does the imaginary become reality? We sometimes create stories, and sometimes stories are created and we don't know where they came from.

The name of Hein makes its appearance again, and

my thoughts return to the man with the watch. There is something about his tragic story that so resembles Faust and his supernatural guide. The comparison is sinister but not overstated. The fear that rested on the quivering words of the man with the watch that makes me think this and also wonder if this guide, the figure who promised to help him with his past and with the child-bearing woman, is the source of a feeling of doom. I am once again knee-deep in a strange darkly dreamy image without explanation, without comprehension, without even a source, but there is something exceptionally peculiar about it: the story persists as though it is happening outside of me, parallel to me, and I am able to grasp it as it unfolds, me with it.

5.

It was the year 1648, and the Thirty Years' War was finally coming to an end, the man with the watch began. I was approaching 60, and I finally felt the weight begin to lift as I witnessed the end to a war that had endured nearly my entire adult life, a war with incalculable origins and that produced unsurpassable devastation: the Great War. As a young man, I had enlisted to go abroad on commission of my brother, working as counsel in Lisbon. I spent years at sea and in the Orient, witness to atrocities without words to match. At the end of the war, I found myself frail and exhausted, aged beyond my years.

And even then afterwards, he continued, I wandered the earth, evading the nameless force of Hein upon me, like a time bomb ticking off my each anxious moment, knowing it would erupt and take me with it. I lived in constant sweats unable to reconcile my incomplete encounter with the girl, distraught, conflicted, agonizing over my inability to undo the past, to make right my fatal mistake. I know now that it has all finally begun to come to an end, the man with the watch explained in lowered tones, to come full circle. It was in that first moment that I looked upon the beautiful, newly constructed Brigittakapelle. Just there, he pointed.

Suddenly floating before his gaze as he stood there at the chapel was a small, worn scrap of paper, resting at his feet. It resembled the old *Flugblätter*, like those that were hung from information boards in the old days announcing strikes, deaths, marriages, changes of estate, such affairs naturally recorded in a town. It's unclear if it came from inside the chapel itself or otherwise had just blown onto its premises by some strange means, but it is as if it were placed there for him centuries ago, though it just appeared, its origin forever uncertain. In that moment, that moment as he chose to pick it up, with a desire not his own and verily despite himself, he felt an indescribable ache both in his heart and the right side of his skull, blurring his vision and causing him to stumble.

There was a long pause.

His voice softened.

For some time, I could not make out the script written on the pamphlet but felt as if I was reading it without eyes. Still not knowing how it came to me, I felt myself visualize the words that repeated in my mind as though entering from another source, like an ancient chant demanding concentration, attention, acquiring power through the rhythm of repetition.

In that moment, his voice became not his own—monotone, haunting, removed from him, from the space of the encounter, of that moment. He took the words from that sinister image on his pallet and gave them their own voice. The man with the watch gestured wildly, his chin lifted, his eyes leaving the space of the encounter. He repeated the very phrase aloud directed at no one, standing there crippled over, ailing and weak, alone in a void on a hazy afternoon before the new stone of the starkly white Brigittakapelle:

Freund Hein läßt sich abwenden nicht mit Gewalt, mit Güte, mit Treu und Bitten.

Startled by its unfamiliarity yet knowing it came from his own mouth, the man with the watch knew it was an ethereal message solely for him.

The words began to come into view upon the page, clear and bright and scripted so finely in his native tongue. He carefully folded the scrap against the door to the chapel and placed it in his satchel, but this gesture instantly caused him to feel such guilt that was somehow connected to the cause of the recently ended destruction of the war. He began to sense that this Freund Hein had always been upon him, an unrecognizable force, for destruction or aid, and he only realized it now—indeed, just moments ago—that he was a fool all those years. He knew he caused his own demise by not heeding Hein's unspoken counsel.

The man with the watch was silent longer now.

The phrase of Hein turned over and over in my mouth without a clear purpose, he began again, though I nevertheless feel myself beginning to understand Hein's role, able more than ever to detect its greater significance, yet still without comprehending the full scene—just there, he pointed again—at Brigittakapelle. My ignorance, howsoever long it has lasted, no longer detracts from my understanding of the message that cannot be changed and is relevant to us all: *Hein can be avoided not with violence, kindness or prayer.*

Through many sleepless and fitful nights, he realized he was sensing this moment, seeing it come, until it had come, and the phrase of Freund Hein came even then again and again on his tongue. He felt it before he even knew of the name itself. *Hein can be avoided not with violence, kindness or prayer.* If Hein is inevitable, this revelation of a name, a figure, at Brigittakapelle might finally offer the chance to repair something. Perhaps the destruction of the war or the loss of his future bride or of the child? —neither violence, kindness nor prayer…

In time frozen, the man with the watch began to explain the war and what brought him to seek solace there at the newly constructed Brigittakapelle on the day of his discovery of the first reference to Hein in print, of what he had hoped to be a numinous encounter to rewrite his past, yet sensing within his body a perpetual dread of the conclusion of the entire intervention, the manifestation of Hein, of Hein on his very own lips, knowing somehow as well that his own mortal fate rested upon the encounter in its fulfillment—and perhaps mine too.

He began his tale by speaking of the temple destructions on Swami Rock during the Great War, what we now call the Thirty Years' War, and how this affected the course of his life.

6.

I had felt myself suspended there in the present moment of time of the man with the watch. Something was telling me that his story would soon culminate, and I again felt myself projected back through his eyes to that spot, rigid, calcified on the stone in front of the Brigittakapelle. I am connected somewhere through the senses as he felt them, as they were being felt in that moment. My own head was thick and throbbing the next morning, and I remained in a cloudy haze that day and the next. I spent much of that time wandering the narrow streets and alleyways of Paris, looking up at the chalky grey buildings with their metal, blue roofs. The stark half moon clearly visible through the fragments of cloud, creating a contrast of light and dark in the imaginary space where their edge meets the sky.

It wasn't long after the insect circus that I returned to Paris. Everyone always asks why I came or returned or stayed. There is no answer anymore. Everyone thinks that it's Paris where you go when you need to enter into the mystery of your own life that is really another life. When you need to enter the mystery that should be your life when you've read about it as some one else's life. None of us know why we've come here, but we are here for the moment. There's a floating, vague sense of what the original reason had been, but it is clouded over by the reality of being in the city, buying bread, fighting crowds, managing affairs.

Most of the people you interact with have forgotten why they are here and not somewhere else or never really had a good explanation in words and so forget in another sense. Those who are here and were never anywhere else expect a kind of living that is only real in Paris, where, as Henry Miller says, *the toilet is always out of order* and *the shutters go up with a bang*. It's impossible, though, to take this for granted if you're not really from here. Maybe this is why we are in Paris.

For a reason unknown I started to I feel a strong urge to uncover my Prussian connection, and in looking through family papers, I came across a letter written to my mother that my brother had given me after she passed away and which I had forgotten or misplaced, but in any case I had never been much concerned with its contents until now. It was dated July 17, 1979, sent from the *Statistisches Bundesamt*, the Office of Vital Statistics, alerting the recipient to the results of a requested search conducted by the *Verein für Familienforschung in Preußen*, the Society for Family Research in Prussia. The letter indicated that, based on the information provided by the recipient and its subsequent relation to information received by the bureau from the *Verein*, that the recipient could claim ancestry in the region of West Prussia, though unfortunately more detailed information could no longer be found.

My mother is on my mind in a parallel sense with the man with the watch, intersecting somewhere, detached or wholly reattached. It has made me want to uncover her entire mysterious life, her childhood in rural Michigan, her escape to Ohio, her sailor and her ten children, her escape first from him and later from them (from us) and her last days in Montana. The question above all that I need to answer is why it feels so urgent, such an imminence pressing upon me and this quest.

It is in these connected darkly dreamy images that I am beginning to feel how I occupy a role that would play a not insignificant part in the final destiny of the man with the watch himself, or perhaps the role that he would play in mine.

Captain January II

Something was clearly amiss. They were sitting at the table in LouAnn's kitchen, a small house on 11th St. near the center of town. Shirt could hear LouAnn's mom vacuuming upstairs. It was Saturday, and Shirt always ate her lunch with great pleasure at LouAnn's on Saturdays, but today she was acting strange. Aloof and dispirited, Shirt was concentrating with palpable excess on the triangle sandwich wedge between her hands in her lap. The two girls had been friends since the first grade but couldn't have been more different than day and night. LouAnn was oblivious to Shirt's discomfort.

'Shirt! You'll never guess! My ma'amee bought me that gorgeous skirt from Malley's just like I've been asking! Isn't it just gorgeous?' She stood up quickly, drawing out the syllables of 'gorgeous' into a singsong growl, as she twirled around on the linoleum, her bright yellow skirt floating upward like a giant spinning parasol in the center of the room. 'Gorgeous!' She repeated.

Shirt feigned a smile, her eyes darting around the room and eventually out of the kitchen window to the horse in the far pasture to the truck coming down the lane to anything outside that space. She felt alone and anxious, and the longer LouAnn spoke, the more Shirt felt herself being pulled down a long, dark tunnel back back back away from the world from reality from any sense of care or attachment.

Without so much as glancing at her companion, LouAnn carried on with her rhetorical inquisition, asking one question after another, all the while picking mindlessly and uselessly at her lunch and making sure her curls, shoestrings and polished nails were in their proper place. 'Shirt! Did you see Jo Johnson's new crew cut?' Once again drawing out the last words of her question like a piece of pink bubblegum pulled between her teeth and fingers. 'Oh, I think it's just horrible!' She continued. 'What was he thinking? I just think his ears are so big and silly!' LouAnn squealed and jiggled in her seat picking up her linen napkin, which had fallen to the floor in her excitement, and placing it neatly back in her lap.

'Shirt! Can you tell me what Mr. Parmali assigned for math? I had to skip after Mary Beth forgot her new lipstick in the ladies room, since I promised I would help her retrieve it. Well, and you know, by the time we'd done all that, well, gosh, it would have been too silly to show up to math so late! Everyone would have found me atrocious in the doorway!' LouAnn rambled on, voice bouncing, high and sharp, but her words were a slow, deep blur in Shirt's ears.

Shirt began to feel the sadness that comes from knowing some one you care about doesn't need you in the same way. It was a feeling she long had but wasn't entirely aware of, though it permanently made her feel displaced. She missed gramps with her heart and her ma without knowing, and all she felt now was a loneliness that over the course of her lunch was becoming resentment. LouAnn was her best friend, and yet she couldn't even see that Shirt was despairing, agonizing over something tremendous. Her own best friend! Shirt tried to look up, but she just frowned, a lump growing in her throat. She had the urge to run away as usual, but she could never figure out where.

'Shirt! Shall we go play records? I saw Bobby Harris at the diner last night. Oh, bother him! You know he's still sore that I broke it off with him last week. That boy needs to grow up. Besides, I've got my eyes set on Jeremy Nelson! Oh, but Shirt, you know Jeremy is dating that awful Sasha Owen. Good grief, but never mind her. I'll make my move, like I do! Don't you worry!' It was as though LouAnn was on stage, entertaining an audience of admirers. She had always played the part, and usually Shirt was among the best of the starry-eyed in the first row, but not today. She used to wonder how LouAnn got on so well with the boys. Sure, some of the girls in class called her 'fast', but what did they know? (And what did that mean anyway?) LouAnn was pretty and kind and from a good family and had a mind to do whatever she wanted. Shirt admired that, but today she was low and was lower still that LouAnn could see none of it.

Shirt finally looked up, making eye contact. Tears began falling.

LouAnn had enormous, round brown eyes, which were now even rounder and more enormous. She blinked and dropped her jaw slightly, making the shallow of her cheeks take on a shadow below the bone.

Caught off guard, she cut short the chatter. 'Shirt! What on earth is the matter?' She finally asked. LouAnn was neither malicious nor conceited, but she was a simple girl who couldn't tell you which way the sun set. Shirt had an accidental mentor and confidant in LouAnn, something she couldn't get at home, and LouAnn had a faithful fan and a ticket to decent grades. She was taken by surprise.

'Shirt! My love! What really is the matter?' Her voice expanded and took on a motherly yet still hollow tone. Though her heart was genuinely full of care, her capacity was an act.

Nevertheless, Shirt already began to feel soothed, her anxiety abating, and the tears streamed more steadily, freely now that help was at hand.

'Oh no,' LouAnn's voice lowered, and she became serious, her body closing in toward Shirt like a mother hen. 'Don't tell me. Something happened with Donny Raleigh. Did it, it did.'

Shirt couldn't restrain herself any longer. 'Oh, LouAnn! He tried to kiss me!' She blurted out. LouAnn froze for half a second, shocked and confused by what she just heard, then she squealed again and a big grin spread across her face. Shirt was mortified, trying to keep herself from finishing the story, but the words fell out before she could stop them. 'And you know what I did, LouAnn? I ran straight across the football field and out of sight as fast as I could!'

LouAnn tried to disguise her giggling. 'You!' she exclaimed, both accusatory and astonished.

Shirt was aghast. What did LouAnn find so funny? The encounter had been horrible. Shirt looked away, not quite knowing what to do or say. She searched for the right expression. She was beginning to feel embarrassed by her feelings now and her actions then. After all, LouAnn knew best. Why did she feel so wrong about it? Her expressions changed rapidly between what she really felt, forlorn, disheartened, dirty, to what she thought she was meant to feel, though she couldn't put her finger on what that was supposed to be. Her eyes darted more wildly. She attempted to smile, but it only made the corners of her mouth draw downward more sharply, more painfully.

Shirt didn't know what to say, so she just said what she felt. 'LouAnn, what am I going do on Monday? What if he tries again? Oh, I just don't know. I just don't know.'

LouAnn's surprised look became stern, and she suddenly sat rigid. 'Oh, girl.' She drew out the Oh, her voice deepening. She leaned in toward the table, her blouse pressing against the edge forcing the buttons to work harder to stay together, the lacy fringe of her undergarments showing through. Her voice lowered, 'Shirt, what's the matter with you? Why you acting so surprised he tried? You're a pretty young thing! He should be so lucky! You need to go for it, honey!' She paused, then adding with a childish earnestness: 'And then let him buy you some presents.' Shirt just stared at her, trying to take it in, take in her miscalculated behavior, take in what she should be doing though it felt fearsome.

'It always works!' LouAnn added with a sideways grin and a wink.

Shirt couldn't fathom that kind of intimacy. It scared the living daylights out of her. There would be nothing genuine about her behaving that way, and LouAnn's reason for doing it felt foul and dishonest, but somehow, Shirt imagined having some impetus of an even more sordid sort would be the only way she could let herself get close to anybody in that way.

LouAnn's face tensed, and she looked at the withered Shirt with a dead seriousness. 'Oh, but you just wait until your Eva finds out, and then you'll know what a good mess you've got into!' She laughed straight away and gave another wink. 'That old witch!'

When Eva's name came up, Shirt felt an ominous grey storm come over the roof of her mind. She looked down into her lap again, played with the crumbs of wheat bread speckled across her skirt. 'Never you mind her,' she said curtly, defiant.

Shirt looked outside. Seen through the water-stained panes of the kitchen window, the sky was a translucent blue with a tenuous strip of cloud suspended within it like a drawn-out cotton ball pulled across rough construction paper. The air hung thick between them for just a moment. 'Sorry, honey.' Like a confession. And LouAnn really was sorry. Her jokes were not always well placed.

The misstep and apology were all Shirt needed to bring herself back into LouAnn's comfortable territory. 'Never mind.' She let the cloud lift a bit, waited, and with as much false drama as she could muster said, 'LouAnn, girl! What am I do?' They were in the 6th grade, and Shirt certainly hadn't hardly begun even thinking about boys, much less get kissed by them.

LouAnn playfully grabbed Shirt's sweater and blurted, 'What was it like, Shirt? Tell me! I want to know all the details,' drawing out the all as usual with great enthusiasm.

Shirt hadn't much to tell. She had been terrified. She had agreed to go steady with Donny Raleigh exactly four days ago. Steve Murphy passed a note in English to her that, covertly hand by hand, had steadily come via the back row from Donny across the room. Shirt opened it cautiously, quietly, making sure the noise of the paper did not call the teacher's attention. She knew what it would say, her gut fell, and fell again when she read the words she'd partly longed to read. Before she could fold it once, she found herself glancing across the room in search of him, and there was Donny Raleigh waiting for her answer in real time. She felt her gut fall again into her knickers. Without even thinking, without even knowing what she was doing, Shirt nodded her head, quickly looking away with an involuntary half-grin on her lips, and Donny nodded back securing the unspoken pact. That day and the rest of the week that followed, Shirt avoided him as best she could.

'LouAnn, what am I going to do?' This time she needed a real answer.

'Oh doll.' LouAnn dismissed Shirt's anxiety. 'There is nothing to be so worried about with boys. You just take charge and show him what you got.' LouAnn shimmied her waist like a belly-dancer and winked with lips puckered.

Shirt had no idea what she meant. She was working hard to understand.

LouAnn also appeared now to be working hard in thought. Her eyes went dreamy as she stared into nowhere; she lifted her chin with her jaw clenched, a gesture marking her effort to concentrate. Shirt took the opportunity to consider her options:

- Break up with Donny immediately.
- Let him kiss her. (It could be somewhere dark enough where he wouldn't notice LouAnn as her stand-in?)
- Avoid him until the end of the school year.
- Change schools.

She knew she would do whatever LouAnn told her, and so it was promptly decided she would let him try again.

'You owe it to yourself to get some experience! Shirt, everything's been taken away from you. This is your chance to get what you deserve. Let him treat you nice. You'll see. You'll like it. It's a nice feeling to be adored.'

Yes, I imagine it is. Shirt thought. She had no idea what it could mean.

'It's time you became the enchantress you are and share with all the girls who are counting on you to tell them what it's like, to know, to share the experience, the wild mystery, take the frightening leap into that exciting and new but terrifying world! Enjoy yourself, Shirt, and take what's yours!' LouAnn was bouncing in her seat with excitement.

The weekend passed without incident, slow as molasses. Despite her decision, on Monday she was sure to arrive at school as the bell rang so as not to have any extra time lingering in the hall. She also stayed late after each class and quickly scurried to the next. English was the last period of the day, and her insides were all twisted up knowing she would see Donny there, imagining her fate, impossibly trying to imagine what would happen next.

Shirt walked into the classroom with her head down turning down the second aisle and taking her seat two rows back without looking up. Out of the corner of her eye, she saw his seat empty. And then filled. She gasped, hoping no one heard her. She dared not look. The lesson began. She felt nauseous and sweaty the whole way through, not turning her head in any direction, barely able to pay attention to the teacher.

55 minutes later, she was gathering up her things and quickly shuffling toward the door. She could feel his eyes on her, behind her, following her, patient, heavy, knowing. She made her way through the halls, to her locker, gathered her books for homework and headed toward the side hall entrance. She let out a sigh of relief; she was feeling light, that she had escaped. She was almost there.

Suddenly his form filled the archway, loomed, overtook her entire space, the voices around her vanished, the halls completely darkened and her gaze narrowed in on the light emanating from one sole point in the building. There he was, coming toward her. Menacing, grinning, shy, like a sheep, like a fox, like a wolf.

For a moment the world briefly opened back up. There were students coming and going, shuffling, yelling, laughing, complaining, in groups in pairs, giggling, tossing balls, dropping papers, closing notebooks. The final bell of the day rang out. He pushed up against her, head turned to the side. She could smell his warm breath. There was no time to move to consider to flee. No words exchanged.

Suddenly she felt a sharp pain in her breast. She looked down in time to see his thumb and forefinger twisted, turning, twisting her nipple between them. She was paralyzed and horrified, and all in an instant as he quickly moved past, she slashed down the corridor running from the school hot tears streaming. Oh god. Oh god. It was all a blur. It was all much worse than she could have ever possibly imagined.

LouAnn called out to her from the lawn. Shirt ran. She could hear LouAnn calling her name, running after her. She ran all the way home and into gramp's empty coop. She hadn't gone in there since he'd died so many years ago. She had nowhere to go. Shirt was overwhelmed with fear. He got hold of her breast, her nipple, he twisted it, he did the deed. She cried all night long. Now she knew: she was pregnant.

Memory and Remembrance

1.

We had climbed a vast mountain and were gazing out over a valley of lakes. It was serene but frightening and was shattered by a piercing cry let out by my brother. I ran frantically up the jagged ledge, which was really like a flight of stairs in an old house where we once lived, to find him sitting in front of a computer with a single-line message from mom: *lose yourself as lovers lose themselves.*

I read it too, standing there behind my brother, also perplexed and silent. She had died already two years ago now. An incomprehensible thought of my own passed through my mind: *She was crying, falling one by one.*

I opened my eyes. Little pink petals were raining down from the cherry tree in front of me. Millions of tiny, penny-shaped, flesh-colored petals. It was 8:30AM. The sky was acting like it was 6:30 or even 5:30AM. It was cold and gray in a way where the grayness itself was causing the cold. It was a day that said, It's good to be loved. The day was blank and cold and unsteady. An unsteadiness. A day that said, You need to be loved today.

I can't be sure if my mom loved me. She was not there when I was a baby and not there again when I was a child and finally not there when I was an adult, and now she has died and is gone. Loving and showing love are not the same thing.

Life needs to be more organized. On its own. Without me. I want to be able to glance at life and understand its structure as something separate from what I impose upon it. Separate from what I understand, how I behave, what I do. I think we all assume this is happening already, because it is too much to have to live in the world but also to have to create it too. I overflow with ideas and feelings and senses, and it's too much to have to recognize there is no start or finish. I am constantly firing off rockets in my head, so many at once. They do not fall into any organized plan on their own, though I want them to, though they need to. I need them to. I don't know how to make sense of the circuitous life of my mother, and there is no place to register my own experiences somewhere as the sum product for a day or an hour or a lifetime or a minute. It's always just going and doing—and going nowhere. It goes nowhere. I cannot log it, because it can't be logged. Not to say that I cannot, but that we cannot. In fact, logging is not the problem. It can actually be pleasurable, though life's array of affairs is always incomplete and vast, and if you find a way to share what you have, you may save yourself the agony of the aloneness of being so strange and alone with thoughts firing off thousands per moment. Because you can share it and know it and live with another.

I am sure the sequence of darkly dreamy images coming to me from the man with the watch are telling me something, something about myself, and I can believe that now, because something is changing, physically changing, and the images themselves are strong, clear, magnetic. These rockets in my head point toward nuances of existence, of the physical world around me, of simultaneously holding every image and memory of the past, every possibility of the future in my mind. I cannot control this, who I am. Even my body is changing. Something is changing. I am not my own.

The horizon has shifted. My eyes are drawn to the impenetrable gloom of the Paris sky in winter. I daydream a labyrinth that I navigate to the end, discovering finally the purpose of the dreams of my mother and of the man with the watch. Moments later, the sun can't be stared at anymore. It's there coming out of the grayness. I drift on to milder thoughts.

2.

During the first free weekend in Mongolia, I went to Tarej National Park with several of the other foreign workers. We were driven in to Ulaanbaatar, and a young Mongolian girl showed us where to wait for the bus. We stood on the corner of a busy main street with a large crowd, a young woman and her baby, several old men with canes and old, ripped coats, a handful of young children tugging at their mothers' skirts with dirty tears streaked down their faces. Buses, taxis, cars missing doors or headlights, honking, merging, flowing, slowly driving past, the dust from the half-paved road kicking up, settling in eyes, on shoulders, a soft layer of sand on everyone's hair and hands and belongings.

Our bus arrived, and we boarded with a large group of locals heading out at the end of the day with their empty milk jugs brought in from remote grassy plateaus each day to sell their contents. It was a clean, modern bus with high seats and room for everyone. We got on the major highway and escaped the overcrowded local roads of the city. Driving into the countryside in the opposite direction from the farm, we saw endless yurt shantytowns, which is where most Mongolians live—huddled up in small, tent-like structures, usually without electricity and without water. Each grouping of some thirty yurts had a well where the inhabitants retrieved bucketfuls of water for drinking and washing. The toilet was a hole in the ground outside the gathering.

After an hour, we left Ulaanbaatar behind, though shantytowns remained scattered about the country-side. On the edge of the city as we passed out were gas stations with fueling tanks lying above ground, large Russian letters strewn across their bodies, one-room, shack-like restaurants identifiable with a *karaoke* sign, World War II trucks donated by the British filling up ditches, billboards of misty skinned Calvin Klein models alongside starched-collared Air China flight attendants.

We arrived at a bridge that the bus did not cross for its size. The locals gathered their belongings, and the rest of us disembarked and followed them across the bridge, empty jugs, babies, baskets, tools, ropes, bags, packages. We walked single-file along the edge of the bridge as ancient motorbikes and old tractors crossed over letting up dust from the unpaved road.

On the other side of the bridge we met up with our transfer bus, small, local, rickety. Everyone patiently waited to climb aboard, taking up every seat, sometimes two children or an old woman and child sharing one seat. An official collected our 2,800 Tugrik for the journey, equivalent to about two American Dollars. I shared a seat with a Japanese girl. We sat across from an old man with a well-fitting, dirty suit, missing teeth and the eyes of the history of the world. Before him sat a teenage couple with their baby and milk jugs. They shared a bright blue, sugary drink, and one by one, during the remaining one and a half hour journey into the heart of Tarej, the baby fell asleep on the lap of the mother, the mother fell asleep on the shoulder of the father, the father fell asleep on the mother, his crown touching hers.

The bus cruised along for an hour until a small stall in the center of the road came into view. We were crossing through a border checkpoint. The passengers sat patiently, and the bus driver paid the fare into the park. The engine started up again, roaring like a beast as we maneuvered the turns and small bridges with growing mountains towering on either side. Eventually, the bus crawled up to the first stop, and the locals exited in twos and threes. With no idea where to exit ourselves, we just waited until the end, when most folks got off. A few locals remained there on the edge of the dirt road, watching as we descended the front door of the bus one by one with our packs and dusty boots and hats. Some comments were exchanged between them, an old woman nodded, several children smiled shifting their eyes quickly from us to one another, to the green hills and the ground before their feet. A few women approached us, stepping directly forward without hesitation while gesturing and pointing across a long field on to a hillside, where we could just barely make out a cluster of yurts. We seemed to be engaged in bargaining. We agreed to 7,000 Tugrik per night per guest, which included a salty rice porridge in the morning, and we followed an old woman and her daughter and grandson across an enormous green prairie with leaping dogs and a wide-angled view down the valley and up to the edge of the forest.

It was freezing. The old woman entered the yurt that had the only burning stove, quickly shooting several sentences through the dark, which seemed to convey that she had brought paying guests home. Suddenly, there appeared a young woman and two young men who began to prepare our yurts. We shared no common language but communicated with gestures, and they demonstrated how we should search the nearby woods for kindling.

The men prepared our stoves and chimneys, and the young woman prepared our beds. Several small, smudge-faced children who had been playing outside followed us around with angelic wonder in their eyes and sideways grins across their weather-beaten cheeks. They helped us find the best locations in the forest for the largest piles of dry kindling—white, twisted rods littering the bottom of the canopy, which served as the only available firewood. We lugged endless armloads back to the yurts, and it sufficed.

As the sun began to set, we made off towards the meager village, consisting of ten or twenty shacks down at the other end of the enormous prairie. We crossed by several yurts, with wild buffalo grazing, horses, dogs and children with one shoe missing. We crossed through the school, with its simple playground consisting of a short set of metal bars from which to swing. We came upon the one room shop, which was attached to another room that had the expected karaoke sign. Out front stood three Mongolian men, watching us as we watched them, in their well-worn Mongolian hats and shoes, their horses tied up to the hitching post. Several children came by on half-functioning bikes, two a piece, a pony pulling a cart with a boy at the reins, another running alongside managing little kicks on an old soccer ball. We walked straight through the village in about ten seconds. When we reached the other end, there stood another one room store attached to a one room restaurant.

We sat down to eat a dinner of whatever they had to offer. It was a small room, in which in one corner stood an enormous pot and a commercial-sized freezer. Gesticulating wildly, we conveyed our hunger. The two women and boy pulled out the only contents from the freezer: frozen mutton dumplings. After more nonsensical gesticulating, it became clear that each person would receive four dumplings and with ketchup. We ate by candlelight. They gave us tea after dinner, which was the same brand we had already been drinking on the farm. It was a means to drink safe water but was itself horrible and, like everything else in Mongolia, tasted like mutton and blown dust.

It was a pleasure to sit in that room, with the two women and the boy and the Mongolian cowboy in one corner engaging our company, looking at us, though I felt it was not in the usual way when foreign. They did not perceive an insurmountable distance. I had the opposite sensation. We were in their room, which meant we were together, and we belonged together. After many thanks and the usual communication confusion, we left their company, everyone gleaming with wide smiles full of wonder and joy and incredible amazement at the very possibility of one another, watching the world expand and contract in an instant.

We returned across that enormous plain, now in complete darkness. The sky reminded us that we were alive and electric in its bright, nearly painful clarity. It spoke to us of the temples in Hohhot and the Gobi desert and the equestrian statue of Genghis Khan rising 40 meters high, not far away. Every step taken in that country under that sky was as bold and timid as flying a kite after a long illness. The brisk air on the cheeks, the gentle pad of the grass underfoot, the alert, tender eyes, the coarseness of everything gliding through fingers, the fragile body longing both for warmth, comfort, the *not yet! not yet!* and new life, vigor, deep, long breath and outstretched limbs reaching for endless heights.

We pressed cautiously, yet firmly upon mossy, peacock earth and cinnamon terrain as we walked, blinking in time with the flicker of the stars—the same transcending, upward-rising glow, moving from burnt orange and cool teal to a deep, ocean indigo. A miraculous, unexpected flash in my mind set me squarely in Montana under the same vast, cold, enveloping sky, sitting around a campfire with my mom and brothers and sisters, singing harmonies, mostly folk tunes, sometimes old war songs like the Andrew Sisters or a Shirley Temple number jibing my mom her namesake, brothers strumming guitar, children running and playing, dogs barking, the tips of pine trees fiercely still on the edge of the world gazing in on us, severe yet gentle against the dark blues of the horizon—and me, somewhere in there. Observing, somehow living.

3.

As pagan holidays, like the origins of *Walpurgis-nacht*, eventually came to be adopted by church institutions, altering them into both secular and religious celebrations—as in the case of midsummer, May Day and Easter—glorifying their origins became more sinister in nature, shown by Goethe in the imaginary. As May Day was itself considered the first day of summer in pre-Christian times, midsummer was set in late June, or what would now be considered the beginning of summer.

St. Walpurgis Abend stands prominently in my mind, as it was the year of the first mentioning of the celebration of *Walpurgis* in the 1603 edition of Johann Coler's *Calendarium perpetuum*, the man with the watch had explained to me, when he first saw the young woman whom he would finally meet five years later with the intention of a proposal. It was at that encounter that he was to transfer the fantastic key to her.

However, when the year arrived and the date arrived for this event to occur and the fateful encounter between them took place, he did not concede. The key was not yet in his possession then, and so in his fear he somehow already knew he would be altering an agenda set for him, in order to produce this marriage and possible heir, as he had thought, and in so doing he thought he would be risking something far greater than what the scene presented.

When the man with the watch did meet the woman

five years later, it may have resembled Faust's last encounter with Gretchen in her cell. Yet it was this momentous reunion between the woman and the man with the watch that ultimately did not produce the union, or so it seemed, 42 years later, as he had explained. I cannot comprehend why he faltered or how this faltering itself was part of his fate. What the consequences might have been I do not know. I seem to have found myself on a journey that I hope will guide me to the answer.

His 17th Century feels both intangible and fixed. The man with the watch cannot reveal his future to me, because he cannot know it, as he is there in his moment—the way his life and history play out, as though our lives are running together like an endless room of turntables circling around and around, crackling, skipping, releasing precise and delicate vibrations, resetting again and again after the last touch of the needle to the carved, spiraling groove of the record.

4.

Simorgh means *thirty birds* in Persian. They could not have known they would find only themselves, but in doing so, the birds exemplify the eternal and universal search of the Great Enigma. It is most exactly the collective self that the birds find. They are not rulers over themselves, but they guide, and that is better.

How do the birds begin their journey? How do they know to become guides? How do they know they will be guides and guides of themselves, but themselves as a whole as a whole collective that is one? We might say it is unconscious. The birds begin their journey because the journey has begun, and that is to say, they are alive, and being alive is a looking a moving an investigation into the alive itself. They are looking for the reason for their being alive. They are looking for their leader. They are thinking for themselves. They are already looking for themselves. Because they fly, they are guided and guiding without knowing themselves as guides but are each in a constant state of motion that is a leading and a following. The eyes the nostrils the cap of their skulls lead them in and through the moist, cool air. Their claws and rumps and the tips of their wings follow, trusting, mindless, enacting unthinking gestures until they are linked, and their skulls provide the destination, but it is not known until it is reached and their wingtips learn it and the shapes that they are and that separate them fall away at that moment.

The justice that the victims of the Haymarket Massacre received offers the same message through the torment of our perpetual quest for understanding, for making things as they should be, and as they should be understood. The victims sought the collective self in the practical—through unionizing, becoming their path to martyrdom. It is their accidental sacrifice for the right to govern oneself that the martyrs acquired their own spiritual collective self. They are delivered to their spiritual unity—how they are perceived and have been perceived since their untimely deaths. They continue to serve as the emblem for the rights of the worker, of the vulnerable individual as bonded in the brotherhood of collective power, like the snake extending his body for the travelers to pass. The Haymarket victims are also to be remembered as a collective unity. They died together and exist eternally together spiritually.

I think of my Joyce book, and I realize its passing to me is another connection, but most would say *Oida versus birds* is a challenge to believe, being read out of a text – produced from a text – that contains its own text. *Oida versus birds* is a creation on the inside flap of a text, resulting in the great mystification of thought and writing. Such writing, strangely, is meant to come from a certain stability of the power and strength of words as they stand, while at the same time it is always the case that where it leads is also a newly mysterious stability: the collective self – the collective self of the text itself and of the reader upon it.

Whitman says, *I am integral with you, I too am of one phase and of all phases*, and *I am with you, you men and women of a generation, or ever so many generations hence*, and most of all—

> *What is it then between us?*

> *What is the count of the scores or hundreds of years between us?*

> *Whatever it is, it avails not—distance avails not, and place avails not*

The man with the watch feels both that Hein is somehow linked to him through this sense of collective unity, but the very thought brings a terror to him, unable to fathom how it could either be true or not imply something unduly ominous and disturbing. I have thought the same thing. What is Hein? If I already knew, I had no clarity of it. If I knew not at all, I was petrified to find out.

5.

I'm concerned about the poet of *The Conference of the Birds*, because it is this source that seems to be revealed to the poet and given to the reader but which the poet composes. It is this source that makes all the difference in what path we choose, or what path we are given, when we read the text. How could he know? Is it the writer who knows? It is only the writer who speculates aloud. And it is this very speculation that becomes possibility, that becomes theory, that eventually becomes spirituality, that becomes the collective self.

The collective self is also composed of a body of individuals sharing not only an experience but recognizing their communality through that experience and hence their singularity as a unity as a result, as in the beginning pages of *Mrs. Dalloway*, where the reader is situated in a bustling, interwar London with Mrs. Dalloway off to buy flowers for her party that evening. There is commotion in the busy streets as a car backfires, where it soon becomes evident that it is transporting royalty. Everyone is looking at the motorcar, transfixed, and those lucky enough to be out front of the gates of Buckingham Palace delight and feel the *thrill in their nerves* to be happenstance spectators of the arriving vehicle. The shell-shocked Septimus Warren Smith, however, is transfixed to his spot not by delight but terror, confusion, *as if some horror had come almost to the surface and was about to burst into flames*. His young wife urges him along, though she too is caught up in the spectacle.

The commotion of the car is followed by a commotion in the sky. A collection of characters is mentioned, characters who do not remain present or visible across the novel but instead represent the seemingly random cross-section of Londoners on the streets that late morning, in the next unanticipated observation of an airplane's vapor trail. Letters are produced in the sky from this effervescent plume, and one by one the unknown figures are brought together both in the text and somehow with one another as they occupy the vast space of London under the sky of the message in vapor and collectively but individually attempt to read out the writing left behind as the airplane moves through the vacant space.

Like small children first learning to read, they each concentrate, devote all their attention, mouth the shapes they see. One gazer mutters that it is an advertisement for toffee. Another figure then reads *Kreemo*, and another *Glaxo*—perhaps part of the same message, perhaps particular brands of toffee. Septimus, on the other hand, considers the sky writing to be a message for him directly. *They are signaling to me*, he thinks. And yet he cannot read the language, in fact he does not consider the message actual words. It is simply *this beauty, this exquisite beauty*. Tears stream down his face as looks up at the vaporous smoke in the sky—

> bestowing upon him, in their inexhaustible charity and laughing goodness, one shape after another of unimaginable beauty and signaling their intention to provide him, for nothing, for ever, for looking merely, with beauty, more beauty!

As I passed by the kitchen window this morning, I caught a glimpse of a large, suspended white blimp as it floated effortlessly through my entire field of vision, across the effervescent horizon, grainy and gritty, sailing quickly, though with an aloof sort of lumber, through the white February sky that colored everything in an impenetrable grayness. Sacre Coeur looming large in the background, as white and seraphic as the speeding balloon itself overshadowed its majesty, having been built of travertine, a stone that constantly radiates calcite, allowing the basilica to maintain its eternal whiteness.

We embark on Septimus' tears of joy for the beauty of the *inexhaustible charity and laughing goodness* of the shapes in the sky. We are given to the collective experience both that he feels in the encounter, his eye with the shapes, and of the other figures reading a distinctly different message—but then also finally the collective force of our shaped experience as the reader, wondering how to dissect or penetrate Woolf's meaning among the diverging visions, knowing that what she gives us is one part of an encounter and yet that exists as a whole in the moment of our joining, firstly with Septimus and the others, but then with her and the other readers—and even finally, with our own lives through the mirror that she provides.

Slowly crossing my field of vision, the blimp, billowing and enormous yet infinitely minute in perspective, reminds me of that era in which I never lived, in which technological advancements included aeronautics, radio and mechanized war. A period shortly before Woolf's *Dalloway*, belonging to Woolf's own life and her circle of friends, of artists, philosophers, scientists, family and neighbors including Ludwig Wittgenstein, tangential but significant figure of Woolf's Bloomsbury Group, who, before becoming the foremost philosopher of the 20th Century, undertook aeronautical studies after receiving his degree in mechanical engineering from the *Technisiche Hochschule* in Berlin in the year 1908. He set off for Manchester to complete a doctorate in the field, having already invented his own kind of airplane as well as a new airplane propeller operated by miniature engines at its tips. Introduced to Bertrand Russell at this time and made familiar to the Bloomsbury circle, Wittgenstein abandoned engineering, first for mathematics and then philosophy.

We might imagine Wittgenstein re-imagining the world, imagining the world as something he could discover through its recreation. Wittgenstein found himself able to dissect the world, to take it apart down to the possibilities of its language, but in his re-imagining, Wittgenstein also found himself plagued by this discovery. As he re-imagined the not-vacuous core of the world of its entire absence, he no longer knew how to bare the necessity of all other explanations given up to that point. He wanted to dispense with metaphysics, but such a gesture, he knew, would remain an impossibility. Even Wittgenstein needed metaphysics in order to set up his philosophy of the death of metaphysics, or, as he explains of his reader at the end of the *Tractatus* in 1918: *Er muss sozusagen die Leiter wegwerfen, nachdem er auf ihr hinaufgestiegen ist.* He must so to speak throw away the ladder, after he has climbed up on it.

Wittgenstein first visited Gottlob Frege in Austria in 1911 to ask permission to become a philosopher. He had chosen to abandon mechanical engineering and wanted the approval of the revered philosopher in this new field to validate his shift. He was promptly rejected but evidently not deterred. Frege asked him to call again after a proper education in the field, and Wittgenstein made his way to Cambridge where he quickly usurped his own masters – Russell, Moore, years later submitting the *Tractatus* as his doctoral thesis in order to qualify legitimately for his already-given teaching post. Frank Plumpton Ramsey had originally translated the *Tractatus* into English many years prior as a teenager and student of Wittgenstein's and now peculiarly held the post of Director of Studies in Mathematics at King's College, awarding Wittgenstein his degree so many years later.

Earlier, Wittgenstein had left Cambridge in 1913 to research in peace in Norway, ultimately struggling the rest of his life to find a way to live a minimalist, rural existence while still working within various branches of mathematics and philosophy that inherently require a dynamic community. It was only after he had become one of the wealthiest men of his day through inheritance (dispensing with the entire sum by 1919 through donation to artists like Rilke, Kokoschka, Loos, Trakl and dividing the rest up amongst his siblings), had fought in World War I (receiving several medals for bravery), served a year in an Italian POW camp, worked as a gardener in a monastery, and trained for, became and resigned as a rural primary school teacher that Wittgenstein was coaxed to return to Cambridge in 1929 to finish his degree. Despite not even having a bachelor's degree from the school, Wittgenstein was granted the Ph.D. based on the theory both that his previous time in Cambridge was sufficient to serve as the full bachelor-to-doctoral coursework, and that his one and only published work, the *Tractatus* (1921), was sufficient to serve as his student thesis. Ramsey was 25 years old at the time of Wittgenstein's conferral and died unexpectedly the following year from an illness of the liver, leaving behind a wife and two daughters.

Wittgenstein lost his faith in god as a young man, turning toward Schopenhauer's epistemological idealism, which asserts that the world is known through experiential perception and hence is only a representation, since we are restricted to the mental pictures of our own consciousness by which to know anything. Once Wittgenstein discovered Frege and mathematics, he gave up on Schopenhauer's metaphysics, though he retained a certain spiritualism that is evident in his minimalist lifestyle, his interest in the arts, in peace and simple living. Paradoxically, however, Wittgenstein could not cease to operate from within a very complex vision of the world, philosophy and the arts, spending as long as two years perfecting his design for the door handles and radiators in his sister's Viennese town-house, now as then considered to be one of the greatest examples of modern architecture.

What was it that Wittgenstein saw after learning of the death of his beloved David Pinsent in a flying accident, his third brother's suicide, the death of his uncle who gave him a home while he wrote the *Tractatus,* the destruction of WWI? Wittgenstein saw with his own eyes and even through the lens of the gas masks what exists between fellow men. In a similar plight, the man with the watch tried to explain how he felt many years after he had left the young woman, why he had left her or had not engaged with her as he had planned as he thought he would, and then experienced the entire European continent fall to the devastation of the Thirty Years' War.

If we can learn through Goethe how to accept not simply the necessity of the individual's sacrifice in the name of the collective, but both the value of the individual's expression within a collective self and the identification of the individual through that collective unity, if we can understand the distinction between the individual ego and its struggle for recognition while transforming that energy into a modest appreciation of its value as one source of light that is part of a greater sending out of wholeness through the collection, perhaps it is here that we'll find a new sense of the value and purpose of our individual expressions within the framework that supports it, defines it and is defined by it, acknowledges and promotes it, without the sense of loss or struggle.

As Aleida Assman explains, *Erinnerung* is notably distinct from *Gedächtnis* in the German language. Translated as 'remembrance', the former, refers to actual, individual experiences, while 'memory', the latter as translated, derives from the passage of thought, or thoughtfulness, observed and adopted, referring to a collective self, a collection of rituals that connect a body to its past, or that define a past to that body collectively. While *Erinnerung* may be affected by cultural forces, *Gedächtnis* is constituted and directly passed on culturally, and it is the cultural forces themselves that are circularly defined by the *Gedächtnis* as it builds and shifts, repairs, accommodates, transforms. *Gedächtnis* is created and defined through media, bodies at work, collective forces of power at work.

Wittgenstein pitted himself against *Gedächtnis* hoping to survive the atrocities he experienced privately, outrunning them or removing them by removing himself, but he could not outrun his own human loss, or the loss of his need to connect to something greater than his own *Erinnerung* that is caused through such isolation, just as the man with the watch could not escape his path within the world that was constructed around him or that he unconsciously yet powerfully constructed around himself. Wittgenstein could not escape and was forced to return to society, having tried to abscond to a small Austrian village, but even then he still could never reconcile himself to the *Gedächtnis* of post-war England with what saw through the eyes of the gas masks.

I think the man with the watch knows something strikingly similar.

I might know it too.

I'm remembering an encounter some time ago working in the soup kitchen in Seattle. I had a long conversation with an old, broken but spirited guy who had moved to the United States from his native France when he was seven years old. He learned a new language and forged a new identity. He told me about Vietnam and his military service in Germany, and how Jacques is Jim in English. It was a lively place, the soup kitchen, and I enjoyed talking with the patrons and hearing their stories, feeling connected for the first time in years with my own past, the years spent in dirty bars and old restaurant kitchens while mom worked and had her drinks. The young guy who ran the kitchen was humble and bright, and I wonder now still how the thoughts connected behind his radiant eyes, doing this work with his life, making jokes about Faulkner and Plato as easily as he'd tell the teenage volunteers a story to get them laughing, striking up spontaneous tunes on a beat-up guitar or explaining to the patrons where to find a repurposed plastic container to take a helping of potato salad home while listening to their long, painful and often senseless stories of hardship or how to peel an orange or get a seat on the bus while it's moving or what granny did with the hard candies left over from the holidays.

How does individual memory perish and cultural remain? The man with the watch shared with me his

Erinnerungen, and because of our separation in space and time, I can understand how the world around me only knows the *Gedächtnis* of the time period of the man with the watch. Impossibly, it is up to me individually, to all of us individually to retain those memories for the sake of something to hold close, for the sake of connecting to the continuum that we are, that I am with the man with the watch, that we each are with one another and that is otherwise impossible to sustain.

How could I keep alive the story of the man with the watch? How can I find and sustain the stories of my mother? Each individual story of each individual accounts for something exceptional, what is unique and distinct, and ultimately lost or at least lost in its transformation into the greater history into which it is woven—not simply to become a minute fragment of that whole fabric but into the very quality of that fabric, the fragment's own unique experience vanishing, as Richard Dawkins says of the way in which genes collaborate to produce the very tangible characteristics of living beings: *It is not the case that each word of the recipe corresponds to a different morsel of the dish.*

6.

Sitting by the side of the river as I often do during short winter afternoons, I watched the barges divide the waves like great beasts gliding across the top of the water penetrating the ripples with the magnitude that I felt of the moment. The barges carry their contents deep within their lengthy bodies, resting far below the surface of the water, creating an optical illusion of being underwater while afloat. I was thinking about the man with the watch, how he looked, his clothing that felt both ancient and quite new, his long beard and mustache, his dark wavy hair with ribbons of grey, the key he held and the small leather satchel. I was thinking about what I knew about the satchel he always carried with him since that day he met the young woman in 1608. More than a dozen years later, in 1622, he nearly lost it at sea, or we might say it was nearly lost to the sea at Swami Rock. By 1650, when he begged the two girls for aid and transferred to them the key, the satchel was still there, tattered but retaining its contents.

This was my own first image of it, by memory through sleep. The man with the watch explained what he carried there inside was the key and that slip of parchment symbolic of his first mention and memory of Hein. The passage of time was distorted as he encountered it through his life with this sinister figure he only came to recognize in 1650 at Brigittakapelle. It was as though he was still in that moment, that moment of recognition, finally acknowledging the path of his life leading to this event, this realization, an admittance of all the lost or destroyed encounters across his life that he sought to recover or change, it all came down to this revelation of Hein, of the presence of Hein in front of him and finally on his lips, jotted down on an old note, quickly tucked into his satchel. Perhaps other objects were there in the satchel too, perhaps relics or something of his own, something I know nothing about, can know nothing about but that nevertheless support an invisible structure of the universe, of each passing instant within them, compressed into each atom.

After the discovery at Brigittekapelle, the man with the watch, as he said, understood that Hein was always with him, his life long, nameless but as an instructive voice turning over in his mind, year after year, preparing him for what he wished, what he asked for but what he knew was beyond his own individual power. Hein gave him strength coupled with fear, and he felt nevertheless instinctively that he must trust Hein, knowing that a power emanated from something beyond what he could articulate, what he could know from his own experiences.

Hein silently instructed the man with the watch concerning the key when he least expected it as he sought refuge in the South Seas, and he knew it was to be his betrothed's though he still could not understand its actual purpose. After all, it was not a ring but a key.

The man with the watch became more tense, less stable and peculiarly detached and anxious as he relayed his story to me, a story that had ceased being a story but became an explanation of the present moment, all life compressed, and I with my eyes closed, mouth open, breathing deeply.

I knew when I was meant to encounter the young woman, the man with the watch spoke slowly, but shortly before we came to cross paths, I struggled to free myself, afraid I was mistaken by fault of Hein, that I had falsely entrusted my future to Hein. But no, I discovered, my mistake was much later, and it was a mistake of doubt. All in an instant, though many years later, I have finally understood—all in my presence of the key, being weighted by the key, sensing it speak to me, guide me, give me purpose, one that I aimed toward without realizing.

The man with the watch only sensed it there standing in agony at Brigittakapelle with the name of Hein on his parched and thinning lips.

7.

Staring at the barges on the Seine, I was closer to understanding how the story of the man with the watch was my own enigma. There were still patches where his message appeared missing, or where I was unable to piece it together or to feel as though I had heard the complete tale. I still cannot understand either why he came to me or what I might be able to make of the consequences of giving the key to the two girls or of the significance of the birth of the baby. There he remains at Brigittakapelle in this instant, our instant of communion. Whose destiny does this key hold? In whose hands should it rest? To which door does it enter? The connection that I began to formulate was both in the name of the child birthed in the phone booth, which somehow I knew was also possibly the name of one of the girls to whom the man with the watch believed the key was meant to be given. This fact was clear to me immediately, and this itself gave me an eerie sense that Hein was capable of otherworldly transformations.

Through my interaction with the man with the watch, I knew he was in a moment of great crisis, vainly searching for a release. Was I his way out? Was I meant to help? To change something? To affect his fate? He was searching for Hein in some determinate form, and yet I feared he had already found him but could not fathom it, leading him to this timeless floating, even toward me, wandering amiss, aching for a change likely never to come.

I learned of his ancestors in Prussia, and he hint-
ed at his searches for the elusive figure of Hein deep
in that region, not unlike, it seemed to me, the Swiss
doctor Frankenstein vengefully seeking out his own
creature, over unrelenting mountains and eventually
barren lands and into the northern world of ice. Or was
it the other way around? The very idea of searching
for Hein, maybe this indicated paradoxically how Hein
was even more present, was perhaps always present
and even came into being—in whatever form Hein's
being could constitute—through the search, through
the announcement, through the desire for some kind
of sense of completion or unity.

8.

Originally identified as a region on the coast of the Baltic Sea, Prussia first denoted an ethnic group inhabiting the area that was conquered in the 13th Century by the Teutonic Knights. The Austrian herald Peter von Suchenwirt describes what harshness they used in their treatment of the native pagans who were often retained as slaves. *Their hands tied together, they were led away like hunting dogs.*

> Die hend man in tzu samen pant;
> So fuert man si gepunden
> Gleich den iagunden hunden.

Peter Suchenwirt was a master of interpreting the coats of arms of knights and noblemen and traveled widely to give laudations at the deaths of important figures, directly serving the Duke Albrecht III in his journey to Prussia in 1377. He died in 1395 in Vienna.

The German state of Prussia took its name from this assimilated area, though its own inhabitants were not necessarily descendent from the ethnic Prussians. By the time of the Reformation in the early 16th Century, the Prussian territory had been confined by the Teutonic Knights, with their leader Albert then declared Duke of Prussia, his duchy a fief to Poland. The man with the watch left for the south Pacific when Hohenzollern took control of the region, re-identifying it as Brandenburg-Prussia.

As in so many instances, including in the life of the man with the watch, this transition of Prussia to Brandenburg-Prussia under the crown of Hohenzollern resulted from Prussia's inability to furnish a male heir. Despite his own seven children, Duke Albert Frederick was succeeded by his son-in-law, John Sigismund of Hohenzollern, as neither of his two male children survived infancy. The five girls, however, married, the eldest to John Sigismund, Elector of Brandenburg. It was already in 1611 that John Sigismund served as regent on behalf of the Duke, who had been in declining mental health since that time. Nearly emulating his father-in-law perfectly, John Sigismund had eight children with two sons dead in infancy. The third, George William, thankfully would become his heir less than a year after Sigismund's official inheritance in 1618 of the Prussian duchy, and his own son, Frederick William, would become the 'Great Elector' for his esteemed leadership and military tactics, paving the way for the Prussian duchy to become a kingdom.

This Kingdom of Prussia was founded in 1701, and many years later in 1871, the German Empire was established, when various city-states merged with the kingdom, but by 1918 the Prussian nobility were forced to recognize their powerlessness and abdicate, with Prussia being abolished altogether in 1932, and officially in 1947 after World War II. My family emigrated to the United States during World War I and so in one sense escaped the final demise of their homeland.

9.

My thoughts twist around Prussia, my mother, history—looking for links, for explanation but ultimately for something far less equitable. We all want to be loved. It's not a consolation, but it helps me understand that life itself is about wanting to be loved. There is no remedy, but there is connecting to the human understanding of that need. It is compassion for the suffering of others in the world, the suffering that is one's own, that we see reflected in the faces around us. The remedy is knowledge, to give somehow to the world to lessen your own suffering by lessening it for others.

What could another person give? Can another person give another what a person cannot give to oneself? What strength can we expect from the world? How can we expect another person to be so strong as to love us beyond our ability to love ourselves? I don't know what love my mother could give or if she received any love and so maybe did not know how to give. Rilke says, *Vielleicht ist alles Schreckliche im tiefsten Grunde das Hilflose, das von uns Hilfe will.* Perhaps everything terrible is in its deepest being something helpless that wants help from us.

We can't expect from another person what we ourselves cannot provide. You must have compassion for your own suffering. I'm only now just learning.

Are we all the same person?

We pass in and out of life. We pass in and out of life feeling this sense of permanence about us; we measure the passage of time from a perspective that feels stable but is violated by time's unexpected and radical movement. We say time passes slowly and, when it's passed, we say it went quickly. It affects our calm and our stability. When I say it *affects*, I am already forgetting I created it myself and so am doing the affecting myself. We encounter one another in the world as mysteries, as objects passing through this opaque and thick cloud of time, suspended and yet fundamentally, like time itself, in movement. With each passing day, we come closer to that vague sense of both an end and a beginning. We look to each day as the beginning of a life that is somehow continuous and yet completely detached from anything else, in the sense that it is a guide towards a fulfilled future—this notion, this sense, this feeling, this desire of a fulfilled future. It is also towards an end—the obvious end of death, itself only a concept, as is the beginning, a concept frequently displacing us, which we try to understand as a positive compulsion towards a more meaningful life.

Beware of a sense of the solid, I think. The solid is the myth that we tell ourselves in order to live in this stable continuum. We don't realize the solid is also the abyss that creates stress and struggle, because the solid is not there. What is the solid? The solid is a sense of life as a meaningful endeavor that runs from one end to the other. The solid is a structure to give us purpose, fuel our pursuit, engage our dreams. The solid destroys us by keeping us stagnant in a sense of being that is stilled, leading us to believe that something awaits, there is something permanent to count on, no need to move past the known, take the risk nor envision a life more divine, without control, true to the lack of truth.

The solid is as dead in the water as Katherine Mansfield and Ernest Hemingway. The solid is insomnia. The solid is anxious tears streaming.

10.

The man with the watch traveled to Königsberg after visiting his brother in Lisbon, where in pale sweats he relayed his last years plagued by a still nameless Hein and his eventual evasion of the expected arrangement with the woman. His brother recommended, he demanded, that the man with the watch forget the matter at once and set sail for the Portuguese colonies in the Pacific. It was this journey that resulted in his spending the latter half of the Great War at sea and abroad. His entanglement with the dark foreboding grew, as the elusive figure became evermore inescapable and yet never quite present. It became evident that the man with the watch was somehow searching for the unnameable and not running away, as he had imagined, and it was as though the travails around him were increasing Hein's presence.

Wherever the man with the watch went, Hein was not just one step in front of him—or behind him—but surrounding him, invading him, not directing him but infecting his vision, guiding him toward some unforeseen outcome, dictating the course of atrocities that he experienced regularly. Death fell in on all sides, the worst being the events at Swami Rock followed by the greatest battles of the war itself.

His story echoed in my head, not resonating but reverberating, bouncing off my thoughts, disconnected, still free. I wondered what these details of the life of the man with the watch could mean to me, as my body continued to feel deep change and I reflected on this space between *Gedächtnis* and *Erinnerung*—the particular elements of his life, of his story and his struggle set in relation to what seemed to be random historical facts but which are lifted and transported in some falsely unified manner, to transcend, transfer, transmit a narrative that takes its place across time, shared, remembered, but in no definite way and with no definite source; a rather defeated display of siphoned events or experiences left over to constitute our collective existence together. There are endless fragments of history to read and learn, to piece together, to try and find meaning through them or to accept the meaning that is given to them through their haphazard expression.

As I weaved together my own sense of the narrative of the man with the watch, I began to feel that he might simply have been afraid, is still afraid, of his own creation and his own death, in fear of being lost to oblivion, and so he begged to return somewhere—finding a young bride, re-appropriating his role to the world, and trying again. I also knew though that it wasn't as simple as that or rather, as we choose our paths, the desire is led by any combination or confusion of the *Gedächtnis* and the *Erinnerungen* that we hold. The man with the watch was already living the tragedy of the Thirty Years' War and could envision perhaps the collective *Gedächtnis* to follow—what was lost to it, but even more pertinently, what it revealed of his own hollow, singular existence. He had no companion, no child and was witness to atrocity one upon another. He was given a set of values, how to imagine the past, which swirled around how to calculate the present, and finally to lament what went amiss.

What is the value of an individual existence, both to itself and after it's gone? What could the man with the watch save by trying to rewrite his story? He could not undo the war nor its imprint, but he thought he could make up for this *Gedächtnis* by giving himself finally something to live by. The force of Hein entered his life without invitation, but this desire for meaning, for fulfillment, for acquiescence was invitation enough. And even more strangely, it was the man with the watch himself who invited the presence of Hein seemingly despite himself.

Hein can be avoided not with violence, kindness or prayer.

We all live with Hein, many in a perpetual search, many in the wake of disaster, either to avoid the unavoidable consequences or, equally, to produce different consequences, even circumstances. Hein is neither a force of evil or good. Hein is, and dare I suggest it? Hein is connected to Simorgh, an inescapable component of our experience from nothing into flesh and back out again. Hein arrives both at one's calling and also against it.

Like the birds of Simorgh, we assume our journey outward to be directed toward a unique destination but which is the collective unity of all of our lives intertwined, moving, flocking as disparate but amalgamated entities, brushing wings, inhabiting one space. The compulsion to continue, alone or en masse, is not motivated by what we think, which is our discrete desire for the discovery of a distinct future, of our unique selves in that future, in success, in progression, in enlightenment or salvation. No, it is the reflection of all bodies, the one body, and the recognition of the pool, all in a moment.

To be plagued by Hein, we might imagine the endless numbers of birds that fell off one by one, that could not complete the impossible journey, that fell to tests of endurance, that failed in their vision of confidence of the collective unity. To gaze into the pool and recognize oneself, this might be to recognize the presence of oneself in the composition of entirety. Is Hein reflection or shadow? It is a question of belief or fear. It is a question of Rilke's *zwei Früchte*—the two fruits. *Gegen die Furcht muß man etwas tun, wenn man sie einmal hat.* You must do something about fear once you have it. Rilke writes of the life that is a death within each of us, and the two lives, *die zwei Früchte*, in the pregnant woman. In her large body, her growing body that she protects inside and outside, across which she folds her small, delicate hands, lie two fruit: *ein Kind und ein Tod.* Her gentle manner, her soft, porcelain smile, in this serenity she shows how they grow in her together, a child and a death.

What do we each of us bear? What am I bearing? What did my mother bear? The woman who carries a child within her is not just bearing the two fruits. She is bearing also the two fruits of the child itself, and so she bears three. How many deaths did my mother bear? Ten children and their ten deaths. Eleven deaths. My mother bore ten children and so with them, their ten deaths and also her own.

11.

It has been said that Wittgenstein admired Rilke. It's not clear to what extent Wittgenstein may have read Rilke. We know that Wittgenstein gave a substantial part of his inheritance to the poet, with smaller divisions of that inheritance going to many artists, most of whom were not chosen by Wittgenstein himself but Ludwig von Ficker, essayist, Wittgenstein's publisher and publisher of *Der Brenner*, an art and culture journal to which many writers including Trakl, and Rilke in at least one instance, contributed. In the case of Rilke, it is evident that Wittgenstein had read at least some of his work and that Ficker, in agreement with Rilke, had encouraged Wittgenstein to seek publication of his as-yet unpublished and somewhat problematic *Tractatus* with Insel Verlag after Ficker felt it too great a risk for *Der Brenner*. Even here, however, Ficker remains the contact, and any direct link between Wittgenstein and Rilke is absent.

Many years earlier, in 1897, Rilke met and fell in love with the revolutionary Russian psychoanalyst and writer Lou Salomé, also the object of Nietzsche's affections 15 years prior. While Salomé's relationship with Nietzsche ended badly not long after, hers with Rilke endured beyond their three-year romance, remaining his lifelong correspondent and muse until his death in 1926. It was Salomé who renamed Rilke 'Rainer' from 'René', taught him Russian and brought him to the rich literary and cultural life around her. Salomé was also involved with Freud, having written on the erotic and female sexuality long before ever actually meeting him, and was acquainted with Helene Deutsch, a pupil of Freud's, considered the first psychoanalyst on women, who was born in Austrian Galicia in 1884 but emigrated to America with the rise of Nazi Germany, where she remained until her death at 97 in 1982.

In the *Duino Elegies* Rilke writes: *Denn das Schöne ist nichts / als des Schrecklichen Anfang*—beauty is nothing but the beginning of terror. If we think of the infinite beauty of giving life, of the two fruits growing in the womb of the mother, we wonder about this terror, the terror of birthing the fruit of death while simultaneously of life. Rilke next tells us how we endure this terror, how we revere it, how we embrace it precisely because it is to become our destruction. Beauty is a form of terror, but it is the form that is endurable. We search after beauty, for it is an echo of the abyss, of our own destruction, quietly resting in the sublime.

The presence of beauty is the revelation of terror at the moment of its acceptance or at the level of its tolerance. The birth of beauty is not only the acceptance of the terror but also a recognition of its capacity to destroy, and we take it precisely because of this. It is Black Elk's compelling fear, and it is Hein, the essence of Hein. There is no birth without the birth of death.

When the woman in the telephone booth bore the child, she gave the world the child and also its death. Is this not Hein or the child of Hein, Heinlein? What is it to carry Hein, waiting to be birthed? How do we know when? Hein arrives not by one's choosing.

I picked up my notebook and walked along the quay trying to keep pace with the looming sea vessel making its way out across the closed waters of the city. The air was cool, the sky its usual soft winter grey. My body was warm against the layers of cotton, my nose and cheeks stinging as they met the invisible barrier at each breath. The story of the man with the watch intensified in my mind with his anxiety surrounding me. I knew it soon must come to an end. I thought of him at Brigittakapelle, the note and the remainder of his story. Something inside of me was stirring. I felt a strange excitement but also a nausea. I felt in the grip of something new and frightening—good or bad, I could not say, but connected to this vision of Hein.

We are all born together. We are all living at the same time. We don't recognize this, but the continuity that we sense, separates us from the fragmentation that is really at work. We don't know anyone who *lived before*. They are always living and dying with us.

12.

I walked along the banks letting the frigid air re-awaken my senses. The wet stones underfoot were irregular, and I walked imbalanced against the harsh wind. The twisting river led toward an invisible horizon as I aimed west, broken, leafless trees brushing my right shoulder. The water was brown and unforgiving; waves made their mark along the undersides of archways spanning the old bridges. I tried to imagine Paris during wartime, saturated with troops, arms and a hollow ache like a thousand thunderbolts in everyman's belly.

The Swedish had taken control of the Wolfsschanze region of Vienna and used it to recuperate troops during The Thirty Years' War. As the story goes, Archduke Leopold Wilhelm survived a bombing while praying inside his tent and so had a chapel built at the end of the war in 1650, in gratitude and honor, dedicating it to the Swedish St. Brigitta. It was the same year and in that very spot that Freund Hein was discovered by the man with the watch, that he held in his hand the single verse written on a scrap of paper.

I breathed in and closed my eyes settling in gently against the soft wood of the bench along the water.

Many years prior, just a short time after leaving the young woman, the man with the watch explained, I set off for Lisbon to consult with my brother. My nightmares of a faceless Hein were increasing, and I thought that by abandoning the path I had chosen would be the only way to restore my health, to recuperate my life, to restore order and control. I was mistaken. I was conducted to the girl by my visions of Hein, but the sense of foreboding only increased as I got closer to her, and I knew something unearthly was taking place, which caused me to attempt to interfere and terminate the entire endeavor along with its consequences.

In Lisbon my brother was a counselor involved in the increasing production of sugar in the colony of Brazil. They were coming into extensive riches and began expanding their control in other parts of the world like Southeast Asia, which gave my brother the idea that I would not only be safe on the other side of the world but would be able to comfortably establish myself. As my brother began witnessing my decline first hand, he immediately enlisted me on a voyage to Ceylon, where I could begin to participate in the Portuguese influence there.

I had no notion of my mission or direction, the man with the watch said, but I trusted in my brother and his position of knowledge and power to guide me. I had only hoped to remove myself not only from the plague of Hein but also from the devastation of the war. To travel to the ends of the world was an accepted invitation.

The man with the watch paused briefly.

Yet it oddly made me unable to foresee the destruction that already lay ahead.

Ceylon was itself a target of the war in what seemed a few short years later, and I remained during those worst years of hardship, returning to Europe only after the entirety of the savage fighting had finally ceased.

I found my brother had been taken.

It was only then that I made my way through laborious hazy paths, continuing in the direction to the Brigittakapella, hoping that something would finally aright, that my chance might finally arrive.

As the man with the watch shared his explanations and tried to complete the story, his own story, as he knew it, carried on in circles, running without direction. He faltered and was desperate, unsure, trying to transmit his message, the past, the story as well as he could, though it seemed that at each instance, the more he told, the less present he became, and the more he faded, some spectral apparition.

The air became murky and disturbed at the chapel, and the man with the watch shouted. He began to swoon. *Hein! Hein! Where are you now, bastard?* He wished the nightmarish encounter would aid him in overcoming his life's curse, but as quickly as he pleaded, as the very thought passed through his mind, he admitted in the same instant what he always knew: Hein was his own creation. It was he who wrote the name on the page, uttered the name for the first time. The ominous truth that he had not only for so long been avoiding, but had thought to be the source of the cursed course of his life precisely through his own denial of its course.

The tension was thick around him. His fear was

amiss, his own apprehension and not the force of this unknown Hein directing him, but he learned too late, and strangely he also understood that he spent his life as it was meant.

Do not let it happen to you! His voice moved from calm to shrieking at each new phrase.

It is now time for the key to find its keeper and the lock to be opened!

By whom the man with the watch did not say. My body was restless. My eyes remained closed.

In that last moment and for the last time, he knelt there, gasping, strangely white and gaunt, eyes bulging, at Brigittakapelle in Vienna, the great capital of the Holy Roman Empire in 1650. Through his eyes I saw a vision of the young woman's child grown, towering before him. He lay there on the soft earth, struggling, hesitant, short of breath, not speechless, but crippled by his very speech. One last time, I heard him find the name of the force that had guided him nearly his life long, and with its utterance at that moment, the man with the watch finally surrendered to it. Seeing clearly what had descended upon him, what he first denied, then feared, then trusted, then fled and finally sought, the man with the watch fell silent and still, as Hein claimed him—as happens to each in given time.

As he faded from me, I could hear his last whispers: *Heinlein…Heinlein!*

Book II

CAPTAIN JANUARY III

May 5, 1954

Dear Diary,

I know it's not right to say
and even feel, but I don't love
Eva, and I don't think I ever
did. And soon it will all be
over. How you know that
dear mama died when I was
just six ~~years~~ old giving birth
to sweet Eli. (God bless Eli.
God bless ~~mama~~)

It was too soon ~~that~~
~~father~~ found Eva, though
I know he was needing
some one to help him raise
us four young ~~girls~~. Eva
was never much of a ~~mother~~
though, and it's finally time
that I'll be getting out of
here. I'll be getting out! I'll
~~be~~ having no more of her ~~annoying~~
pulling ways and false smiles
and sly coquetry. Father
doesn't know what she's up to
and what she does to us girls

THE ORIGIN OF VERMILION

either, but we have to stay
good for him. Father needs
her, and I suppose that's
okay. He's got nothing else,
but I'll be getting out of
here as soon as school is
finished tomorrow at noon.
I don't know why the other
girls didn't leave, but they
just didn't and now they're
gone started families. Sara
Jo in Ann Arbor, and well
maybe that's good enough for
them, but I'm not making
that mistake, no ma'am.
I've got plans. I'll be telling
you, as soon as I take
my diploma, I'll be leaving
for good.
I'm going to the city where
LouAnn's got a cousin there,
who told her she'll give me a
place to stay for a while and
with low rent. She might even
be able to help me find a job,
and then soon I'll be able to

enroll in college and get
proper skills like secretarial
and take care of myself all
on my own. Gramps might
even be proud of me and my
dear mother too. (God bless
Gramps)
As a child I wanted so badly
for Eva to be my new mother,
but nothing can replace
your mother. And Eva didn't
even want us. She used us
to fill something up in her,
an emptiness, something she
felt in herself that she
could not change. Despite our
efforts we could do no right
by her. Something was
always amiss, but now
it's over. I will be leaving,
and that's enough.
I've got the timetable right
here, and it looks like there
is a train that connects
near Flint and passes
through little Holly town

before connecting to the Canadian
National Railway and heading
into Detroit. From there I I
can get to Cleveland on the
direct express line. No time
for hesitation now.

Until we're somewhere over the
rainbow,
always yours,
Shirt

May 7, 1954

Dear Diary,

I've finally gotten a chance to write again, and I'm writing from the sheriff's county prison in Cleveland, Ohio! Don't worry. I am fine. Everything is going to be alright, but boy did I have a scare.

The trip to Detroit was dark and cold, and I felt a kind of chill in my heart and was relieved to get away, but then I cried the whole way on the bus from Detroit to Cleveland. Something came over me, and I started to miss Gramps and my papa and my sisters, and just didn't know if what I had done was right. When I got to Cleveland, I went to use the Ladies' Room

at the station, to clean up
and so on. There were a
lot of gals in there,
looking very pretty and
getting fixed up. I
didn't know it, but they
were lady night workers.
They were prostitutes!
Before I even knew what was
happening, there was a
"raid" (a gentleman
explained it to me later),
and all the gals were
arrested, me among them!
The police officer grabbed
me by the arm and
called me a "nasty
enchantress," and before
I knew it, I was put
in their van with those
other poor souls. Not to
worry, though, a nice
gentleman sailor who
I'd sat next to on the bus
is out speaking to the
sheriff right now to help

clear up this whole mess.
He is a kind man named
Peter Roska. I've already
telephoned LouAnn's co_____
and she knows he ___
be bringing me to her, so
I think everything is going
to work out just great.

Yours as always,

THE DANCE OF THE BAY

1.

The viceroy sent a messenger to come find me. I was escorted down complicated old streets to a large hall filled with finery, a long table and a generous feast upon it. The viceroy was sitting at the head of the table smiling at me. Without breaking his gaze, his eyes shining into mine, the viceroy slid out of his seat in order to welcome the true guest and performer, an enchantress. I was never told who she was, but it was said that we had an intimate history together that I couldn't remember. She performed an intricate dance that called to me in a double personage. She fanned her body around, painted, changing form, and though I was somehow moved by the acquiescence, I didn't feel moved in myself. On the contrary, when she spoke through her body, I was disgusted. I dismissed her, and the viceroy came back to the head of the table. I felt pain in his presence. At the moment I needed to escape to find solace, a motionless but kind old woman appeared at the side of the table with her body turned toward me. When I saw her, I felt love, need, familiarity and fell to my knees sobbing into her lap.

I just want to go home, I cried. I just want to find my home.

She comforted me and was gentle and calm.

Have patience, she said. It was my mother.

2.

My head was muddled, my body felt crushed and heavy, and I thought maybe something important was being shown to me, altering me, offering a presence perpetually to tempt me with past desires and maybe even desires yet to come—or rid me of both. Somehow I wasn't stirred, I wasn't stirred either as I thought I would be or as I might have been. Instead I felt a need for something comforting, tangible, warm and loving, like my mother, like a mother, because I never had a mother, and for the comfort of a love that was more primal than any other kind.

Black Elk calls it the 'compelling fear' when, after he had had his own visions as a boy and after his family and many others had to leave their homes and cross many lands because of the white man, he knew he was too weak, timid or afraid to act upon his vision. He couldn't save his people, and he regretted this, what seemed like childhood cowardice, and though he knew he was spoken to by the Grandfathers, he felt he could not speak it or share it.

Still he did share it after much time had passed and he found his courage, he did call out to the Grandfathers in the night sky ten years later or more, still a boy, and after they had fled and all the horses had died and everyone was dying, still he ran and he told his people to flee again, and they did.

Telling the story and lamenting his inability to act or to understand or to accept, an aged Black Elk telling his story, he knew that his story was just one, a part bound up with all the others, a story of the communal link between man, every man and woman and animal, tribe and band, and his visions were not his own but were given to him, not as a prophet, but as a man who was given instructions, a role to play, something greater than one man, than one gesture.

The compelling fear is Black Elk knowing he must express his vision and cannot ignore it or, more importantly, disbelieve it. The compelling fear announces both its unavoidable and grave consequences but also its dire necessity. In what way is self-doubt an instrument of fear but also a recognition of our individual dependence on the community to envision and enact a reliable and meaningful future? Black Elk would never claim any significance of his own tale, as a tale belonging to him, but would give it meaning only through it as an expression of the community, its plight, its history, its future. It is here that Black Elk could find significance in articulating, in sharing, in bringing to light his own role or his collective role, his given role to him from the collective spirit of the Grandfathers in the collective experience of all beings. It is also here in the wide space of the collective experience of life that allowed Black Elk to express the compelling fear, to allow it to manifest in him and to live in its wisdom, to believe in its expression as a collective entity, a collective force, collective significance.

3.

The old story of the man with the watch was washing over me with each passing day, connecting to me to what I already knew but could not fathom, my anxiety about sharing what I saw or felt. Something is transforming inside of me that I don't know yet, but I know it's connected, and I am still waiting to know, to know if I can know, about Hein. The woman in the booth birthed a baby who itself became the figure of Hein, *Heinlein*—finally accounted for and named by the man with the watch so many years later. The rescinded proposal was a highlight of his fear, his inability to live, to live out a life that embraced its own death—bearing the fruit of one's own mortality, as Rilke explains.

I do not feel the way about Hein that the man with the watch felt. I could detect something sad, something impertinent, something falsely fearful in his behavior. He defeated himself, his own life by running from Hein, from the feeling of Hein, from the feeling of knowing of the existence of Hein in his life, what Hein represents or symbolizes. For me it is something else, but I will wait. I can wait for it to arrive as it should when it should, and now with the viceroy and my mother, I sense a link to a new darkly dreamy image, and I can feel the joint between them.

I walked along the river under a thick grey sky, wet and cold, blurring into the edges of the buildings, until my legs were heavy weights, and, exhausted, I sat on a stone bench next to a mangled, ashen tree whose roots were irregularly breaking up the cobblestones around it. Then in the peace of the moment, watching the motion of the waves, passing barges, litter and debris splashing up on the edges of the massive stone banks, I thought about the Thirty Years' War as it was felt across the world, and the destruction there at Koneswaram Temple.

Built many centuries before the Common Era and venerated for over two thousand years, Koneswaram Temple was destroyed in two years under direction of the Viceroy to Portuguese India, Dom Francisco da Gama in 1622, its third and final monument toppled in 1624. Trincomalee, where the temple is located, was the setting of a costly naval battle of the Thirty Years' War. Five hundred Hindu shrines were desecrated during this time, and the destruction of Koneswaram on Swami Rock was itself the largest pillage of any ancient site in history, with thousands of years' worth of valuable and priceless objects looted in an instant. The objects are still intermittently recovered, including the ruins of the temple itself, discovered in 1956 by Arthur C. Clarke, who chanced to emigrate that year to Sri Lanka to learn scuba diving.

During the annual festival of Ther Thiruvilah in 1622, the statue of the Koneswaram temple was paraded through town and consequently ransacked, like an inverted Trojan Horse, by Portuguese soldiers disguised as Iyer priests. In the ensuing chaos over those next days, statues and precious items were buried by the frantic Hindi desperate to save anything in any manner, and the temple itself was cast by the natives into the sea off the cliff as a gesture to retain a sense of purity, of honor in its inevitable destruction. The Danish had already arrived in 1619 at Trincomalee and began building a military structure of their own but were themselves attacked by the Portuguese during the same or similar attack on Swami Rock and the Koneswaram temple under the leadership of General Constantino de Sá de Noronha by command of Philip IV of Spain, also known as Philip III of Portugal.

The newly ascended King Philip IV, whose son was to be the last Hapsburg emperor of Spain, is not especially remembered as a successful king, though he did rule over the Spanish Empire at its height. After many lost infants and the loss of his first young wife, the king married his niece, eventually siring his heir, Charles II of Spain, who was severely disabled, living to age 38 without any children of his own. King Philip IV of Spain is remembered like many members of royalty as a patron of the arts, his daughter or perhaps himself being the subject of Diego Velázquez's masterpiece *Las Meninas*. His young daughter Margaret Theresa of Spain is the *infanta* at the center of the painting, surrounded by her *meninas*, though to call her the subject of the painting might be to miss the complexity of the work. Margaret Theresa died at the age of 21 after six pregnancies and four living children, one surviving infancy, dying at age 23 in 1673.

The subject of Velázquez' *Meninas* is not only a mystery but the subject of analytical interest for historians, cultural and art theorists and anyone interested in the historical shift from classical representation to modern interpretation, as it's generally perceived. Foucault wrote extensively on *Las Meninas* in *Les mots et les choses* in 1966, bringing the work and its depiction into the critical theory arena. Suddenly, according to Foucault, with this masterwork by Velázquez, the age of representation now makes way for the age of meaning and signification: the painting does not simply depict; instead it requires the observer to invest, to analyze, to conclude. This message itself is overtly present, says Foucault, in Velázquez's ambiguous and playful work.

What we learn from Foucault's analysis is that the painting's spatial structure indicates there are particular figures somehow residing outside the painting and yet are, in a seemingly paradoxical manner, literally included in the painting. There are of course two paintings, the one that we see as the spectator of *Las Meninas* and the one that is being painted by the Velázquez within the frame. Looking closely, we observe through the mirror at the back of the room King Philip IV and his second wife and niece Mariana of Austria, the apparent subjects of the painting within the frame. Unexpectedly, we see the painter himself, in the process of representation, and we also see a spectator, not unlike us, the viewer of the process, standing in the doorway. These, as theory tells us, are the three requirements of any work of art—the artist, the creation itself and the audience—and are here included not simply as *representation of representation*, but rather as an introduction to modernity.

There is something behind this canvas, Velázquez taps us on the shoulder and whispers, Foucault explains. Here is the man, the one who is representing. This is not a depiction of reality. This is a construction, and even stranger still, Foucault says, we can only know this through historical change or difference: we see the transformation before Velázquez and through him and out of him. He provokes our own modernity, but he himself does not, cannot, live within it.

4.

With stones thieved from the Hindi and guns from the Danish, King Philip's Portuguese soldiers built the military *Fortalesa de Triquillimale* in place of the once magnificent Koneswaram. By 1639 the fort was already under Dutch control, rebuilt and renamed Fort Fredrick, current home to the Wellesley Lodge installed in the 18th Century in honor of the visiting Duke of Wellington, Arthur Wellesley, when the region was a British colony. The lodge serves as the housing quarters for the volunteer battalion of the Sri Lankan army.

Arthur Wellesley is best known for having defeated Napoleon at Waterloo, and although he was but the first Duke of Wellington, he retains the title popularly despite its technical passage onto his descendents. Wellesley was named so in 1814 by King George III in honor of his military accomplishments, particularly at the Battle of Vitoria of 1813 against the French, which sent Napoleon into exile. This, as is well known, was followed by Napoleon's last effort during the 100 Days in 1815, where he was defeated once and for all at Waterloo by Wellesley once again—lifetime Commander-in-Chief of the British Army with participation in over 60 battles during his life long. Known to never publicly show emotion, Wellesley broke down in tears after the Battle of Waterloo, it is said, having been overcome by grief, his body and heart and will diminished by the high mortal cost of the battle.

Wellesley also gained high regard for his role in the

Sixth Coalition's defeat of the French on behalf of the Spanish during the Peninsular War of the Napoleonic Wars, considered one of the first national wars and the first war with large-scale guerrilla tactics. After Spain and France had allied and invaded Portugal, the French turned on the Spanish, hoping to conquer the entire Iberian Peninsula for itself. The Portuguese however were secured by the British, their subsequently strategic location eventually serving as a stronghold for launching successful attacks against the French, aiding in the Portuguese victory.

If it hadn't been for Napoleon's miscalculation to invade Russia in 1812, he may have been more successful in Spain and Portugal. This kind of speculation, however, undermines the very principle upon which Napoleon conducted his entire campaign and is fallacious. Napoleon's military strategy on the Iberian Peninsula was motivated by his greater desire to conquer the whole of Europe and beyond. The failure of one part would signify failure, or even preemptive stasis, of the entire enterprise. His vision was grand but delusional. The magnitude of the success he hoped to achieve could simply not come to pass but itself would necessarily need to remain an ongoing project— until something broke it free and let it tumble, let it all tumble and undo the end and perhaps elevate the process without understanding that, without the end, it was all a futile disaster. Transformations may be possible, but we always await the fate of all such unreasonable expressions of control.

The single greatest transformation the Portuguese undertook in their 16th and 17th century conquering of the Jaffna kingdom was the full and forced conversion of the Tamil to Catholicism. By 1591 Catholic missionaries were comfortably carrying out their duties, having established an arrangement of tribute with the natives. When in 1617 the usurper king Cankili attempted to modify the political landscape, the Portuguese had him hanged and forced the entire royal family to adopt holy orders, nuns and priests they all became, eliminating any further claimants to the throne. Rebellions took place, citizens fled, and those who remained suffered under the terror of Portuguese colonization. Today Sri Lanka is predominately Buddhist, with a small portion of the western waterfront practicing Catholicism.

Christian tradition claims that Thomas the Apostle arrived in Sri Lanka in the 1st Century and was killed, probably lanced, in Tamil Nadu. What work he might have done is not clear, as it is evident that the Portuguese laid the greatest hand upon Christian conversion in the land. St. Thomas' remains were excavated in the 16th Century by the colonizing Portuguese with inconclusive results.

Like many or all martyrs, the death of St. Thomas the Apostle was gruesome, no less than that of John the Baptist, but there is more detail to John's legend. Gustav Moreau depicts Salomé dancing before the baroque throne of her stepfather, King Herod and his wife, Herodias, Salomé's mother, pleasing him enormously with her intoxicating form and beauty, as was his request. In his infatuation with her body and grace, the king offers his stepdaughter and great-niece anything she desires. We know from the Gospel that, similar to Herod in his improper request, Salomé abuses this offering of power, perhaps at the behest of her mother, and vulgarly demands as payment the head of John the Baptist. Some depictions cast her as regretting this decision, but we see in various interpretations including Oscar Wilde's that she relishes this shameful desire, which is perhaps no more a desire than a rebellion against her stepfather. She becomes the ultimate femme fatale of folklore.

I am reminded of my mother, the temptress who seduced men and took their well-being. She took their money and their credit cards and gave us their dead wives' earrings. She struggled her whole life to take care of her ten kids, but what she chose only made it more severe. She worked in the dirty kitchen of honky-tonk bars. She was feisty and exceptionally beautiful, and the men liked that, so she found a way to get out of them whatever they were willing to give up, but it was never enough and never right and never did anyone any good and never ended well. It didn't end well.

The man with the watch had also hoped to change his story from the inside out, only making it worse, not seeing what he saw already. Not seeing or knowing until it was too late.

I sense their paths running closer together.

5.

During the destruction of the Koneswaram temple, the 16th century Saraswathi Mahal Library of the Nayak Kings of Thanjavur was also destroyed. A recent creation at the time, it may have held less weight of significance than the temples for the Tamil, but it was rebuilt by the 17th Century nonetheless and now contains over 60,000 tomes including many priceless items, palm leaf manuscripts in ancient languages, an original of Dr. Samuel Johnson's dictionary of the English language and other late 18th century rarities, ancient maps and architectural documents, the pictorial charts of the evolution of man as depicted by Charles Le Brun, heralded by the Sun King as the greatest French artist of all time.

Thinking about the paintings of Charles le Brun, examining for example his best-known work, the ceiling of *la Galerie des Glaces*, or Hall of Mirrors, at Versailles, I started wondering how his work is characterized as the greatest in painting ever created, or, more strangely, reported as of the best art, as a matter of historical fact. It's not important whether or not the spectator agrees, since the assessment is made as a historical reference to the overall legitimacy of taste or even of authority of King Louis XIV. Because Le Brun was granted such a title, and by such a venerated figure, this title can only be contested not eradicated. It becomes an observation. There are two elements that strike me in the claim: the first is how art is regarded based on its initial historical judgment, and the second is how our own perceptions are perceived and judged based on historical conventions. You can say you do not admire Le Brun's work, but it will not alter his conventional position. What it will do is place your aesthetic judgment under scrutiny, while leaving Le Brun both his reputation and his name hovering in the room.

Spectator theory in the 20th Century focuses on the distinction between the construction and the content of a work of art, or we might say *surface* and *scene*. Crossing into modern art from classical, Velázquez's *Las Meninas* asks the spectator to recognize the frame of the painting, to analyze it from a distance of recognizing its construction. I am a painting, it says. At the same time, it is representational in its content, such that the spectator views the scene as an actual historical experience and is absorbed by its accurate depiction. Spectator theory in general is registering the balance between entering into a painting, such as one experiences most easily within the classical tradition, and returning to its perimeter to analyze it as an aesthetic object, which is evoked without end in the modern tradition.

Ernst Gombrich argues that the spectator cannot simultaneously see the picture that the painting is trying to convey while also observing the detail of the *strokes and dabs on the canvas*. This balance between the *illusion* of the painting and the *strokes and dabs* collectively make up the aesthetic experience, and for some theorists in disagreement with Gombrich, this twofold nature is not only necessary but indeed composes one phenomenon of surface and scene, necessarily occurring at the same time, which is fundamentally the spectator's visual experience. We move inside and outside the painting with ease.

How an artist comes at the construction of the painting is, according to Gombrich, not simply a question of perception and interpretation but involves what he calls *schemata*. As with our understanding of Charles Le Brun, we create our perceptions of the universe built upon endless systems that came before and that infiltrate and influence us without our awareness or ability to modify. The painter takes these schemata, pairs them with a conscious awareness of the techniques and forms of the old masters, and begins the process of creation through a feedback loop, such that the desired image is made, evaluated, corrected over and over. The starting point of any work of art is really a collection of understandings, unconscious beliefs and histories and a desire to create, which spills out of the artist in all directions.

6.

I tried to imagine again the viceroy grinning at the head of the table, perhaps transmitting orders on to me, to find me, from his kingdom unknown to me. The vision was an indication to let go of the past, to reconcile broken connections and to embrace what I felt was developing inside me and all that came with it. Resuming my walk along the Seine, I thought about the disenchanting enchantress that he had set before me and wondered how often we are confronted with an old desire that has lost its allure its value its significance. Nevertheless, there was something conflicting about the viceroy heading the banquet, presenting an unwanted gift and leaving me with the need to bury my head in the knees of the mother figure. It was conflicting because it contained both my desire and my fear.

I wondered what the beautiful woman sought to enact when she danced before me, and what the double personage might be that I was immediately compelled to reject, and I think of Hein and of my mother and struggled to find a connection, the answer, I always hoped, coming to me from somewhere upon waking. I wondered if that is what the man with the watch had felt when he stood before the Brigittakapelle and discovered that it was he himself who had written *Hein* on the parchment, and so I wondered too why I place the enchantress before me only to fear and reject and place my mother before me only to desire and feel abandoned. Is this too the compelling fear of Black Elk? My body was becoming less my own. As I walked along the medieval river's edge spanned by ancient bridges nearly every 100 or 200 meters, passing La Tour St. Jacques then L'Hôtel de Ville, my body felt foreign, light, almost beyond or separate from me, from my control.

We must permit life to have many different rhythms. The talents of one person are expressed in another. It came upon me recently how we are not individuals in the senses we imagine. We are appendages, reflections, responses, carriers, images of a collective self. It is nothing to say one is successful or enlightened, because we are all of the same experience. It is a collection of performances firing out in bursts of experience, what we see across time, through space. All of the nuances of an individual are but fractals spiraling outward into the galaxy over and over, many the same and intertwined, repeating and sharing, not with any more or less meaning or value, time or bearing. It must also be true that all of the qualities of the individual are cherished, are integral, but are also nothing and are what we must prize, prize collectively, for each part each viewing is sacred simply because it is, and it is part of what is the universe, transferring and shifting across bodies. This is not spirituality but recognition of the universe outside of the ego.

7.

Richard Dawkins explains that the distinction between man's humbling awe toward the sublimity of nature does not preclude religion, spirituality or anything supernatural. Dawkins cites Einstein and Hawking as two significant atheists whose views are often misconstrued as religious in the way that they speak of nature and its power, their use of the word *God* and their personal focus on a poetic naturalism of the cosmos. Wittgenstein, as we know, is always trying to remind us that it is indeed the way in which we talk about things that creates how we believe in them and not the other way around. The language of *God* in the realm of beauty is ready-to-hand and is often evoked regardless of the speaker's personal religious convictions or otherwise. Wittgenstein might say Einstein is not playing a certain *Sprachspiel* correctly when he speaks of *God*, knowing well that when he does, he is not intending to refer to the supreme figure of any imagined or unimagined religious code. It could also be that the listener is not aware of the rules of the *Sprachspiel* used by Einstein and so misconstrues his message, assuming he must be making a reference.

Dawkins gives us the concept of the *meme* to elaborate on the way by which communal beliefs impact how cultures evolve, likening the process on a basic level to genetic evolution. Certain ideas pass with more impact than others, thus validating themselves, though the means by which they are believed and maintained and shared are not fundamental to any inherent validity, but rather to the sequence of events that led to their being adopted and retained over other memes. They exhibit both Darwinian and Lamarckian traits, Dawkins explains. In the Darwinian sense, memes are copied into subsequent generations, and, in the Lamarckian sense, the end result of the meme is adopted and not the process by which it may be achieved. Learning to ride a bicycle does not require pedaling the specific number of rotations your brother pedaled when he taught you, but rather in maintaining a vertical position and propelling yourself forward by the act of pedaling.

In the 18th Century Jean-Baptiste Lamarck researched the possibility of organisms inheriting traits not just through genetics but rather by *soft inheritance*: behavior, through initiating adaptive changes and passing them on to offspring. It has been only recently in modern evolutionary research that Lamarckian inheritance has earned creditability, within the field of epigenetics, which endeavors to prove how changes may occur in evolution by means other than through genetics, or rather other than through DNA modifications. We can say that epigenetics studies heritable changes in gene expression that occur without causing changes in the actual DNA sequence. The idea that non-genetic factors also cause gene behavior to be modified permits any number of possibilities of sources for those changes, but it still remains within the realm of gene expression such as *histone modification* whereby the spools on which the DNA are wound is altered without the DNA itself bring altered. Perhaps it is not what Lamarck had in mind, but such discoveries may serve as humbling reminders that our systems theories are not only ever imperfect, but are necessarily so. We might remember Wittgenstein's ladder.

The speed at which evolution occurs also remains debatable, with Stephen Jay Gould proposing the theory of *punctuated equilibrium* in 1972, suggesting that evolution is generally stable but experiences moments or periods of rapid change, as opposed to *phyletic gradualism*, which explains evolution in terms of a steady, gradual process. Gould also devised a theory of *spandrels* in relation to evolution, asserting that, as in the architectural design of domes, a certain unexpected and yet necessary shape is left over in the corners to accommodate the round top on the structure's angular body. This space, the spandrel, is itself useless in the overall design, but nevertheless becomes filled with painted imagery of its own, hence immediately—and paradoxically pre-determinately—acquiring a purpose, an aesthetic inheritance and value after the fact.

Dawkins is skeptical of Gould's theory, believing instead that all evolutionary changes must indeed have a purpose of their own or would otherwise not occur, but I wonder if he isn't already falling victim to a false kind of reasoning or some form of his own criticism of divine cause and effect, considering, after all, how he ascribes *telos* to pure elements of nature. Indeed, perhaps also paradoxically, Dawkins is opposed to Gould's theory of group selection and altruism in evolution, whereby an organism behaves in favor of the survival of the group in opposition to a solitary insistence on its own. In its grandest form, this would be the Gaia hypothesis, which suggests that all organisms operate fundamentally toward a level of collective harmony or homeostasis.

Examining the purpose of an organism at this level already requires a certain structure of language where we must assume that distinctions need and can be made among what is a neutral expression in genetics; yet that neutral expression is derived from within our own structures of belief that can actually never be neutral, nor can we even comprehend neutrality from outside the concept of perpetual non-neutrality. Are we using the right *Sprachspiel*, and would it even be possible to use another, more correct? This is not really likely or indeed possible, since of course we operate at the level of the functionality of our entire organism, and that includes viewing all levels of being from behind the lens of humanity, regardless of how neutral we would like to see things or how well we would like to create a concept that takes the place of the imperfect one of neutrality. Even this imperfect concept of neutrality itself only exists from within a structure that cannot see what neutrality might be or mean outside of our ability to conceptualize it. As humans, we are unable to envision things as they are outside of us, particularly as they are on a level that requires a different form of expression than we even know how to comprehend, let alone produce.

Stephen Jay Gould turned 60 the day before September 11, 2001. He was already suffering from his second attack of cancer after twenty years free, this time of the lung, from which he would die the following spring. He had overcome a usually-fatal form of abdominal cancer in his 40s, suffering intensely for two years yet proving, through his survival, the seemingly useless abstract nature of statistics. As a campaigner against creationism, Gould advocated approaching science and religion as two distinct fields that simply do not overlap, not unlike Dawkins but with a drier explanation that unexpectedly becomes much more beautiful. We may understand Gould to mean that one can have both a scientific and religious perspective on the world, but more importantly, his account pinpoints how nature does not, because it cannot, provide evidence that would somehow be available through the moral lens of the human. We cannot apply such tools toward mechanisms that require a different mode of operation.

Our failure to discern a universal good does not record any lack of insight or ingenuity, but merely demonstrates that nature contains no moral messages framed in human terms. Morality is a subject for philosophers, theologians, students of the humanities, indeed for all thinking people. The answers will not be read passively from nature; they do not, and cannot, arise from the data of science. The factual state of the world does not teach us how we, with our powers for good and evil, should alter or preserve it in the most ethical manner.

Because we are incapable of viewing the world at large neutrally, we have a difficult time in understanding or even distinguishing between science and religion. Gould tries to show us that a world may exist in itself despite our desire to understand it through our fallible, or at least non-mechanical and hence spiritual or moral, perspective. This lack of ours, however, does not determine the reality of that outer world, and it would provide a clearer and even more sublime appreciation if we could accept the distinction and the relevance of that outer world from within the beauty of our human lens. Recognizing that we are responsible for how the world is viewed and treated reminds us of the responsibility we have to it and all its inhabitants.

When Stephen Jay Gould died, his wife asked Steven Assael to create a deathbed portrait and Eliot Goldfinger a death mask. We revere such objects of our loved ones and the loved ones of others as though they are part of the deceased, in a manner, WJT Mitchell would say, of animism where the objects or images hold a power distinctly of their own; we cherish them and honor them and even fear them, believing in the power they contain in themselves connected to something outside of us, beyond us, a connection to another realm, spiritual or simply to an energy outside of the visible.

In his death, Gould lives for his loved ones through those images, beyond his research for diminishing the metaphysical. We are animals, and we often hope to develop modes to engage both with the physical world and our spiritualizing minds, which exist through something that the *factual state of the world* cannot aid us with.

8.

In 1600 shoemaker Jakob Böhme of Görlitz, Lusatia of the Holy Roman Empire, now Poland, experienced the greatest of a series of mystical visions when he found himself inexplicably riveted by the magnificence of a beam of light reflecting in the shallow base of a pewter dish before him. The moment, he felt, confirmed the existence of a spiritual structure to the universe that repeatedly reveals the inextricable bond between man and god and the presence of good and evil. From this revelation Böhme learned to trust in his spiritual path while continuing to work as a shoemaker, and so he soon began writing of his discovery of the numinous world, eventually believing in a greater, more profound and exacting unity to the cosmos. Upon his grandest vision in 1610 Böhme concluded that he, like Black Elk, had been instructed as an individual toward a special divine path with a collective purpose. For the next 15 years, Böhme wrote mystical texts by hand, circulating them among friends, until his first book came out in 1624, which immediately entrenched him in a scandal of heresy. He fled to Dresden but returned a short time later, after the death of his accuser. He himself died within a few months leaving behind a wife and six children.

Böhme's writing caused controversy, as some of his ideas were radically mystical and contrary to his and his community's Lutheran religion. Christ did not become incarnate to redeem sinners or eradicate sin,

Bohme alleged, but to offer love and embrace humanity with a vision of god as compassionate toward the real human suffering that directly results from having been divinely created. Böhme also believed god's own being necessitated this creation of man, and that through the teachings of Jesus, harmony on earth is possible. Inspiring many later fringe sects as well as visionary poets including Milton, Novalis, Coleridge and Blake, Böhme was also influential upon philosophers including Schelling, Schopenhauer and Hegel. Most significantly, Böhme stressed independent awareness and commitment to personal faith, as opposed to the blind following of doctrine and religious law.

Through Böhme, Schelling declares that the potential harmony of humanity results directly from the act of embodiment of god in the flesh; the struggle and gesture of becoming, of coming into light out of darkness, and within this darkness itself is the *Sehnsucht* to become. Böhme did not believe Christ's human conception was immaculate. The idea of Mary as a virgin he found absurd, and instead emphasized her mortal, human qualities as that which made Christ accessible, *a brother not a stranger*. Böhme proclaims that only through Christ's physical, human conception and growth in the mortal body of Mary does he become holy and known to man, and in this way does his birth and existence fall away from spatial and temporal restraints, and therefore the existence of the believer also falls away from spatial and temporal restraints and so remains ever in eternity.

All things come from the mother, Böhme writes; all birth and creation is through the mother, and so all things perpetually manifest the presence of *mother* in their very essence; mother is illuminated in form and consciousness.

Also auch die Engel können außer ihrer Mutter nicht leben. Even angels cannot live apart from their mother.

I lived apart from my mother; she left when I was a child, and now here I seek her in dreams and in waking dreams and at the table of the viceroy.

In the language of Böhme, light, fire, luminosity are emblems of the relation between man and god, and so we experience through the words of Böhme that the mortal being delights in a *helles Licht*, a bright light, that is brought forth to the *Feuerleben*, the life-fire, of god. I don't know if the life-fire consumes us or if it is to be feared or even if being consumed by it is fearful. Perhaps this *Feuerleben* finally allows the *helles Licht* of mortality to live beyond itself, to grow into a new fruit and carry on out of the past.

Like Rilke's revelation of the terror in beauty and our attraction toward it precisely for that terror, that darkness, mystery and unknown, Schelling elevates the beauty of *Sehnsucht*, the longing, that permeates darkness and allows it to be penetrated by light. Such a *Sehnsucht* is not simply an escape out of darkness into light but an actualization of the one with the other: of the two fruits in the womb—the light, the dark, the child and the death. Perhaps like Blake's contraries.

I wonder about my mother and this *Sehnsucht* that

I might feel towards what is missing but can never be recaptured. I want this darkness to enter the light, but it can only be a forward motion now and nothing to return to. What I rejected at the viceroy's table and what I sought at the feet of my mother suggests I know this to be true and can seek out the path to enact it.

9.

It was a dark grey winter morning in Paris, where as usual not a shred of light permeated the thick overhanging gloom, and I considered walking east along the banks of the Seine for two miles until I reached the Bibliothèque Nationale. I wanted to investigate their extensive collection of ancient pottery, second only to the Louvre, particularly their ceramic vases of Ancient Greece, such as the one described by Keats.

Although the BNF is the national library of France and contains 30 million items, I still somehow find it quite difficult to navigate, with access to materials tightly restricted and complicated, particularly at the François Mitterand location, which resembles and operates like a fortress. I usually end up there more as an exercise to escape the dreary frozen atmosphere outside, inadvertently engaging in their labyrinthian systems of academic research. However, for this particular quest, I ended up heading northwest to the Richelieu location, which also houses the coins, medals and antiques collection.

In 1924 Georges Bataille took up the position of head librarian in the *Département des Médailles* at the BNF Richelieu and, through painter André Masson, befriended the surrealist writer Michel Leiris. Both men fell out with the movement under André Breton several years later and continued to work together on Bataille's journal *Documents*. Drawn to the extreme left, to concepts of sacrifice, excess, death and sexuality, Bataille established the secret society of the *Acéphale*, producing a review from 1936-1939 inspired by the philosophy of Nietzsche. During that time Leiris and Bataille, together with Roger Caillois, founded the *Collège de sociologie* in response to the rise of fascism and took part in such movements as the suppression of slavery in French colonies, the Spanish civil war and, later, the support of Algeria during its war of independence in the mid-1950s.

Bataille died in 1962 from a hardening of the arteries to the brain, having written during his lifetime, like Leiris, both radical fiction and philosophical texts. One of his best known is *L'histoire de l'oeil*, initially labeled pornographic but later recognized as a significant example of the literature of transgression, in its use of a metaphorical and symbolic framework to carry out a stylized philosophical critique of convention, taboo and the nature of writing. Shortly before Bataille's death, Leiris became head of ethnographic research at the CNRS in Paris, publishing on a variety of topics and within multiple genres up until his own death from a heart attack many years later in 1990, including novels, poetry and critical texts on artists, among them a notable account of his friend Francis Bacon.

Aside from being curator in his professional life of the medallions collection at the Bibliothèque Nationale, away from philosophical and anthropological studies, Bataille also conducted research and published on coinage such as his work *Les Monnaies des grands Moghols* (*The Coins of the Great Moguls*). In this work of 1926 we already see a hint of what was to come of Bataille's interest in the rapport between sex and death that began in 1928 with *L'histoire de l'oeil,* where he focuses the text on Mogul rulers' fascination for erotic excess, sacrifice and sanctified violence.

The *Département des Monnaies, médailles et antiques* at the BN includes over half a million medals and coins as well as 35,000 non-monetary objects: cameos, intaglios, Greek vases, ivories, bronzes and other sculptures and inscriptions. The medals section itself contains over 100,000 pieces, allowing the visitor to retrace an entire evolution of the art, including original moldings of works in stone, wood, wax and plaster.

Patrons enter the library on rue Vivienne, turning right once through the information lobby out to the right of the *Salle Ovale* and toward the coins and medals collection. I walked along the external passage with a sense of the empty air around me. I entered the corridor through a large set of doors that creaked when I pulled the right one open and felt a warm draft of musty air cross my face. The place felt abandoned. As I was standing there in the hall staring at the case of rare keys, the memory suddenly struck me, and I knew and wondered how these keys might connect to the man with the watch. It seemed that before me was something I had imagined akin to the very key that he had been holding, had passed to the two girls, had intended to give to the young woman. I also thought of the enchantress and wondered if the key itself as presented to me in the first image of the man with the watch could have been meant for her, or for me there at the table of the viceroy, as an opening to amends with the loss of my mother. Am I also haunted by Hein?

It has been two years since my mother died. She left when I was very young and returned several years before her death. She comes now in dreams, without speech but sometimes with judgment or in comfort.

There were eight artifacts in the case each with a brief description, save one where there was only a photograph in place of the object itself. Outlining the evolution of key and lock-making, the display provided cursory examples for far-reaching historical periods, noting first ancient Egyptian pin-tumblers, Russian and Chinese padlocks, 18th century double-tumbler English locks and 19th century American cylinder locks. What drew my attention was the missing key. Fourth from the right was an image of an old key of magnificent design that recalled those I'd seen from 17th century Europe. Resembling an ancient skeleton key, it looked as though it fit into a warded lock that was also perhaps capable of opening a multitude of locks with vaguely similar wards, and for this reason could be considered a skeleton key. At the same time, it seemed to incorporate more notches than would a skeleton key, and so perhaps for that reason was designed for one sole lock but a lock that led onto subsequent locks with more intricate entrances, such as one might find in a chateau, monastery or other structure that is served with one main entrance followed by multiple, restricted corridors and pathways within its domain.

Either way, this key did not simply open a container or vault but clearly belonged to a compound, likely of some vast design.

I read the description. *Son origine exacte est incertaine. Il est probable que la relique a ouvert des parois extérieures d'un ou de plusieurs des temples hindous détruits au Sri Lanka pendant la guerre de Trente Ans, puisque c'est là qu'elle a été trouvée, bien que son mécanisme soit inconnue dans la région. Elle a été récupérée au cours d'une série de fouilles au 20ème siècle et est une propriété privée, mais a été montrée ici à la bibliothèque, à plusieurs reprises. —Bureau des objets coloniaux de la Renaissance et de l'empire Moghols.* Its exact origin is unclear. The relic is thought to have opened exterior walls of one or more of the Hindu temples destroyed in Sri Lanka during the 30 Years War, since that is where it was found, although its mechanism appears foreign to the region. It was recovered during one in a series of excavations of the early 20th Century. It is privately held but has been shown here at the library on several occasions. —Office of Colonial Objects of the Renaissance and of the Mogul Empire.

For over twenty years, the man with the watch carried an old key perhaps acquired during his service for the Portuguese at Ceylon until he encountered the two girls and begged for their help to restore it to his lost bride. It was the acquisition of the key itself that led the man with the watch to reconsider the proposal to the woman 42 years earlier. It was the key that sent him mad thinking that history was running on a false track.

It was the key that set off the revelation of Hein, Brigittakapelle, the note; but not as the man with the watch supposed. No, his encounters with Hein never took the course he had expected. What could it be then that this key drives its possessor to seek out doors or paths or workings that are not meant to be? Are Hein and the key always opposed? Has the key ever met the lock that it opens? It is just a dirty trick?

I retraced the story. The arrival of Heinlein to the woman in the booth in 1608 signified something sinister for the man with the watch. In 1650 he drew his last breath before the Brigittakapelle before the very presence of Hein, of Heinlein.

No key could ever help the man with the watch unlock a door that is not closed or that does not even exist. Looking at the image of this key here now, I ask myself how any one of us in the world might be able to intervene on behalf of another.

10.

I walked home but immediately felt an anxious suffocation inside, so I set out again to the market. On
the streets before me there were slow and quick figures without limbs without eyes without voices. I felt
a surging pain against my heart, pushing against my
flesh, that ached to fix them, to fix something, to fix the
unfixable. What is goodness? Is it to be 'good' to help?
Is it worse to think there is a place to help? Is pity as bad
as Nietzsche said it was? If human beings desire worth,
value, purpose, companionship, community, then pity
is destructive, serving only to humiliate, to gain lever-
age, to establish power over the pitied. Strength and
power are transferred. Pity positions equality against
subservience. It annihilates strength both in the one
who pities and in the pitied. It poisons health and, as
Nietzsche says, makes suffering contagious. *Das Leiden
selbst wird durch das Mitleiden ansteckend.* Blake found
pity to be divisive, both harmful in its corruption of the
soul but also healing in its ability to unify and create
compassion.

My pity and my goodness are pathetic. It's improb-
able anyone needs me for anything. I conclude from it
that my sense of usefulness or, more particularly, of pity
for the world is not only pointless, but it is a suffering
of my own that has no real object attached to it. The
world goes on before me and after.

The question is how do I, or do I, affect the after?
Is it too much to think so? The 'before' as well. The

man with the watch tells me that I do, unless it is his own mistake to think this is possible. I am beginning to sense that it is the collective self and the mode by which we all engage, which we all interact across time and space. I am not afraid of Hein.

I returned to the library the next day in order to locate the *Bureau des objets coloniaux de la Renaissance et de l'empire Moghols.* The corridor of rooms was still, narrow, windowless, thinly carpeted and dirty. Next to each office was a small placard on which was written the name and subject of each employed inhabitant, yet I don't imagine anyone spent much time here. Its emptiness was thick upon the air, like a perpetual Sunday afternoon. Unsurprisingly, I was there at the wrong time. I would have to return again.

The air and sun falling slower outside, the air inside stagnant, cold and smooth.

11.

The Mogul, or Mughal, Empire spanned the Indian subcontinent from the early 16th Century to the later-mid 18th. The word is the Persian and Arabic form of Mongol, referring to the descendents of Mongolia, whose leaders were holy descendants of Genghis Khan. The Taj Mahal at Agra is one of the many majestic structures erected during the reign of the powerful Shah Jahan of the *golden age of Mughal architecture*. Yet it was during the reign of Aurangzeb that the empire expanded to its greatest, containing a quarter of the world's population, not quite including Ceylon, unable to conquer both it and the southern most tip of the subcontinent, thus leaving the future Sri Lanka to its European colonists, including the Dutch at Colombo, Negapatam and Cochin, and the Danish at Tranquebar. The Marathas warriors may have helped the Europeans keep the Mughals at bay, waging their own three-decade war against the empire in the last quarter of the 17th Century, the longest war in Indian history.

Built as a tomb for the emperor's wife, who died giving birth to the royal couple's 14th child, the Taj Mahal was begun in 1632 and completed in 1653. 15 years earlier and across the world, John Donne's own beloved wife, Anne More, passed away as a result of having just given birth to the couple's 12th child, who also did not survive. He wrote her an elegy, "Since she whom I loved, hath paid her last debt", and many other poems including "Oh, to vex me, contraries meet as one", both considered part of Donne's *Holy Sonnets*.

We might think of Blake when we think of contraries in this way as Donne as written. In *The Marriage of Heaven and Hell* Blake writes:

> *But the following Contraries to these are True*
> *1. Man has no Body distinct from his Soul for that calld*
> *Body is a portion of Soul discernd by the five Senses, the*
> *chief inlets of Soul in this age.*
> *2. Energy is the only life and is from the Body and*
> *Reason is the bound or outward circumference of Energy.*
> *3. Energy is Eternal Delight.*

Though we consider Blake a mystic, he like Donne was interested in the earthbound, in man and the physical body itself. Contraries are in man's nature, a constant pull between diverging forces though not opposing, the concrete and abstract, secular and sacred, the corporal and spiritual, yet always with a focus on the earthly, or, we might say, on pursuit of the divine within the corporeal. Carnality and godliness, union of thought and feeling, forcibly bringing together the earthly with the sublime—alleged dichotomies that instead, in Blake's development, are bound and necessitate and incorporate one another. They are not dualities but essential and obliging contraries, existing in support of one another, not as opposites but as working interdependent forces. *As infinite, as none.* Eternal and mortal.

12.

In Mongolia came that feeling of connecting sky and earth. We woke up in our sleeping bags on top of the brightly orange-painted wooden yurt bedframes that first day in Tarej to a serving of the sour and salty rice porridge. The day was windy, and we set out with a loaf of the preservative-laden, round bread and a large bottle of water, passing over that somehow expanding prairie, into the village. On the western edge of the village, the way our bus had come, there was an uninhabited luxury hotel built a decade ago when democratic prosperity seemed at hand. We followed along the edge of its crumbling sand volleyball court, where we saw a fallen tree used to cross the river. We traversed slowly, the gently raging waves below, next walking through a small forest that opened out onto a very large plain, much dryer and flatter than the tremendous hill near our camp. We stayed near the trees at the edge of the river to follow its path, with the plain on our right, hoping it would lead us directly toward the next valley.

The wind picked up. We walked in the bright sun with the current harsh against our faces. We walked sometimes in silence and in laughter. We passed three calves lying in the path, two yurts far off in the distance on our right with a Jeep out front and one sandy child chasing another. We carefully passed a bull, next a group of wild horses grazing near the river. The strangely coarse wind was nearly intolerable. After walking for over four hours, we were losing hope of reaching the next valley that day. The trees grew thicker around us, and suddenly we saw a darchor, a Buddhist prayer flag. It is said that the flags disseminate compassion and strength through the wind, sending nothing above or below but evenly throughout. We would have good luck if we circled it silently chanting our communal, yet unvoiced, wish.

We reached the end of the path, or the edge of the valley, or the river turned in a new direction. To go further meant climbing up an incline, away from the river and into a very dense wood. On the hilltop ahead was the first person we'd seen in hours. There sat a boy on a horse with a large herd of goats. He looked 10 years old. Another boy was leaping barefoot from rock to rock, as the goats themselves did. We sat down under a tree on the soft, padded ground, exhausted. We ate chunks of our dry bread, washing it down with the fresh water. We were fools. We had a bar of chocolate, and this was given to the boy on the horse. We stood to go back. We stretched, we ached. We walked back down towards the river. We looked up and saw a rainbow encircling the sun. There was not a cloud in the sky. It was bright and cold, sunny and windy. We gazed unmoving, then moving, we looked at one another, we laughed, we stumbled, trying to keep our balance while staring upwards.

When we reached the river, an old man with a young girl on an ox cart offered to carry us across. We hopped aboard, nearly soaking our feet as the waves came up above the wheels. The little girl giggled and ogled us. On the other side we offered the man some Tugrik, which he kindly accepted. We entered the small village and went into the sole little shop, where we had a cup of tea. It warmed us back up, its flavor bitter and dirty. The entire afternoon was still ahead, so we ventured out and found a young man who offered us a horseback ride. We paid a modest sum and mounted our horses. I was asked to lead the way, the others escorted by their reins. He told me to cross the river first and he would follow behind. I moved slowly without shifting my gaze and watched the water climb to my stirrups but no higher. I did not look back. I did not know what was behind me.

Once I was on land again, I galloped ahead as the others followed, woven together as a pack. We rode back up the old path we had come down and into the forest. We saw more yurts, other children, horses, golden yellow hills, trees shooting up around us sporadically, tall grass, abandoned fences, an old cottage, goats and cows and sheep.

We returned to our camp where the Mongolian family had prepared us a warm dinner of noodles and carrots and cabbage smothered in a brown sauce. Afterwards we played card games and word games, games of trust and memory, eating the sweet, biscuit-like cookies and sipping tiny cups of bright Mongolian vodka. The fire burned effusively and we stepped outside and gazed into the longing, clustered sky, wordless songless cold bright and gentle Mongolia sky that sky that takes us in its arms flooding us with a sense of awe of comfort but also of sublimity vacillating from controlled fear to exuberant joy letting us know it has been before and always will be after and what we are is spread across that expanse and is to be cherished, cherished in the sense that we must cherish ourselves never to be forgotten or forsaken.

13.

Born Arjumand Bano Begum, Mumtaz Mahal received her known name from Mughal emperor Shah Jahan and was considered his most beloved of three wives. Though she was his first betrothed, the couple married a long five years later upon astrological counsel for a happy marriage. In the interim, the emperor married a Hindu princess, fathering a daughter who died in infancy. Niece of the Persian Empress Nur Jehan, Mumtaz Mahal also became the emperor's trusted companion and advisor. He permitted her unprecedented power, giving her authority over the imperial seal for final approval of official documents. The emperor was deeply grieved upon her death at age 38, needing to be coaxed from a year-long seclusion by his eldest daughter, Jahanara, who became First Lady after her mother's death, herself also undertaking significant political roles.

Jahanara was known for her financial support for the building of mosques and her personal devotion to aiding the poor. Her work transformed the city of Shah-jahanabad, including the construction of the Chandni Chowk bazaar, completed like most of her projects in 1650. She is said to have been well educated and highly artistic though her work has never been recovered. We imbue her legacy with that kind of power of reputation that requires our unconscious trust, marked not by doubt but by mystery and a gentle, sweet melancholy.

Dom Francisco da Gama was the great grandson of

notorious explorer Vasco de Gama and was first named viceroy to Goa by King Phillip II in 1597, serving until 1600 and again from 1622 to 1628, when Portuguese settlements were under intermittent, yet costly and successful, attacks from both Emperor Shah Jahan and the Maratha. Despite de Gama's best defenses, Ormuz was taken in 1622 by the Maratha, which was also when Trincomalee was equally plundered by Viceroy de Gama himself. It was as though each side chose both a simultaneous offense and defense, both losing more in the process than gaining. After de Gama's return to Portugal, the emperor himself took Hugli in 1629 along with 1,000 Portuguese as prisoners, whose final end we can only imagine.

It is possible to consider the role the Mughals might play united with the Maratha against the Portuguese. We might consider them employing the Bedouin philosophy of brotherhood, but I ask myself about the possibility of brotherhood at such a level as we see in betrayal in war. I don't think that alliance in war is the same as the link of alliance from the individual to the family, tribe and nation, or beyond or within. I am reminded how for Böhme the divine is found first in the carnal inception of Christ as *a brother not a stranger*, which suggests that what we all seek in the brotherhood of alliance is not an allegiance against an enemy or stranger but the revelation of our own divinity, such as was discovered by the birds of Simorgh. Our ability to actualize the divine through our collectivity out of our very flesh recalls the mother, and so again, we see in Simorgh the revelation of the mother but which is only found in the mirroring reflection of each of us, collectively.

The light of the divine emanates from embracing our mortal flesh and from our awareness of the fire that illuminates our existence, the *Feuerleben* and the gentle, bright light, the *helles Licht*. The light is fueled through the celebration of our mortality, which is transformed into the divine precisely because it is birthed out of the carnal, producing its eternity—spaceless, timeless. Goethe's snake recalls the same sentiment, as when the snake encounters the four kings who spontaneously interrogate it on its existence. The snake begins by explaining its mortal delivery from the earthen mother, which is where the gold resides.

–   *Wo kommst du her?*
–   *Aus den Klüften in denen das Gold wohnt.*

The snake announces that more divine than gold is the luminous.

–   *Was ist herrlicher als Gold?*
–   *Das Licht.*

When asked for the source of the light, or of our ability to know it, or even more so, our desire for greater illumination, greater refreshment, greater enlightenment than light, the snake offers language.

–   *Was ist erquicklicher als Licht?*
–   *Das Gespräch.*

Captain January IV

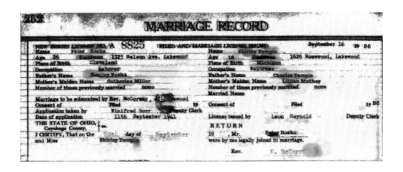

STATE OF OHIO
OFFICE OF VITAL STATISTICS

CERTIFICATION OF BIRTH

STATE FILE NUMBER	1957-200134	**DATE RECORD FILED**	OCT 3, 1957
NAME	BETTY ROSKA		
DATE OF BIRTH	OCT. 2, 1957	**SEX**	FEMALE
BIRTHPLACE	OHIO		
MOTHER"S NAME	SHIRLEY ROSKA	**FATHER'S NAME**	PETER ROSKA
MAIDEN NAME	TEMPLE		
MOTHER'S BIRTHPLACE	MICHIGAN	**FATHER'S BIRTHPLACE**	OHIO

Note: LEGAL NAME CHANGE ON FILE or BIRTH AFFIDAVIT ON FILE CORRECTING [Filed Flagged Fields from Birth Affidavit] or Delayed Birth Record. File date is correct.

This is a true certification of the name and birth facts as recorded in the Office of Vital Statistics, Columbus, Ohio. Witness my signature and seal of the Department of Health this [Date] <format DD/MM/YYYY for date printed>

State Registrar of Vital Statistics

APPENDIX DD
3701-04-1003

DETACH AT PERFORATION

VERIFY PRESENCE OF DEM WATERMARK   HOLD TO LIGHT TO VIEW

STATE OF OHIO
OFFICE OF VITAL STATISTICS

CERTIFICATION OF BIRTH

STATE FILE NUMBER	1959-200490	**DATE RECORD FILED**	MAY 10, 1959
NAME	AMBER ROSKA		
DATE OF BIRTH	MAY 9, 1959	**SEX**	FEMALE
BIRTHPLACE	OHIO		
MOTHER'S NAME	SHIRLEY ROSKA	**FATHER'S NAME**	PETER ROSKA
MAIDEN NAME	TEMPLE		
MOTHER'S BIRTHPLACE	MICHIGAN	**FATHER'S BIRTHPLACE**	OHIO

Note: LEGAL NAME CHANGE ON FILE or BIRTH AFFIDAVIT ON FILE CORRECTING [Filed Flagged Fields from Birth Affidavit] or Delayed Birth Record: File date is correct.

This is a true certification of the name and birth facts as recorded in the Office of Vital Statistics, Columbus, Ohio. Witness my signature and seal of the Department of Health this [Date] <format DD/MM/YYYY for date printed>

State Registrar of Vital Statistics

APPENDIX DD
3701-04-1003

VERIFY PRESENCE OF DEM WATERMARK   HOLD TO LIGHT TO VIEW

STATE OF OHIO
OFFICE OF VITAL STATISTICS

CERTIFICATION OF BIRTH

STATE FILE NUMBER	1961-200018	**DATE RECORD FILED**	SEPT 18, 1961
NAME	LYNN ROSKA		
DATE OF BIRTH	SEPT. 17, 1961	**SEX**	FEMALE
BIRTHPLACE	OHIO		
MOTHER'S NAME	SHIRLEY ROSKA	**FATHER'S NAME**	PETER ROSKA
MAIDEN NAME	TEMPLE		
MOTHER'S BIRTHPLACE	MICHIGAN	**FATHER'S BIRTHPLACE**	OHIO

Note: LEGAL NAME CHANGE ON FILE or BIRTH AFFIDAVIT ON FILE CORRECTING [Filed Flagged Fields from Birth Affidavit] or Delayed Birth Record: File date is correct.

This is a true certification of the name and birth facts as recorded in the Office of Vital Statistics, Columbus, Ohio. Witness my signature and seal of the Department of Health this [Date] <format DD/MM/YYYY for date printed>

State Registrar of Vital Statistics

APPENDIX DD
3701-04-1003

DETACH AT PERFORATIONS

VERIFY PRESENCE OF OON WATERMARK — HOLD TO LIGHT TO VIEW

STATE OF OHIO
OFFICE OF VITAL STATISTICS

CERTIFICATION OF BIRTH

STATE FILE NUMBER	1962-399001	DATE RECORD FILED	SEPT. 18, 1962
NAME	PETER ROSKA, JR.		
DATE OF BIRTH	SEPT. 17, 1962	SEX	MALE
BIRTHPLACE	OHIO		
MOTHER'S NAME MAIDEN NAME	SHIRLEY ROSKA TEMPLE	FATHER'S NAME	PETER ROSKA
MOTHER'S BIRTHPLACE	MICHIGAN	FATHER'S BIRTHPLACE	OHIO

Note: LEGAL NAME CHANGE ON FILE or BIRTH AFFIDAVIT ON FILE CORRECTING [Filed Flagged Fields from Birth Affidavit] or Delayed Birth Record: File date is correct.

This is a true certification of the name and birth facts as recorded in the Office of Vital Statistics, Columbus, Ohio. Witness my signature and seal of the Department of Health this [Date] <format DD/MM/YYYY for date printed>

State Registrar of Vital Statistics

DETACH AT PERFORATIONS

VERIFY PRESENCE OF OON WATERMARK — HOLD TO LIGHT TO VIEW

STATE OF OHIO
OFFICE OF VITAL STATISTICS

CERTIFICATION OF BIRTH

STATE FILE NUMBER	1964-873038	DATE RECORD FILED	APRIL 2, 1964
NAME	CHARLES ROSKA		
DATE OF BIRTH	APRIL 24, 1964	SEX	MALE
BIRTHPLACE	OHIO		
MOTHER'S NAME MAIDEN NAME	SHIRLEY ROSKA TEMPLE	FATHER'S NAME	PETER ROSKA
MOTHER'S BIRTHPLACE	MICHIGAN	FATHER'S BIRTHPLACE	OHIO

Note: LEGAL NAME CHANGE ON FILE or BIRTH AFFIDAVIT ON FILE CORRECTING [Filed Flagged Fields from Birth Affidavit] or Delayed Birth Record: File date is correct.

This is a true certification of the name and birth facts as recorded in the Office of Vital Statistics, Columbus, Ohio. Witness my signature and seal of the Department of Health this [Date] <format DD/MM/YYYY for date printed>

State Registrar of Vital Statistics

APPENDIX DD
3701-04-1003

DETACH AT PERFORATION

VERIFY PRESENCE OF DOH WATERMARK   HOLD TO LIGHT TO VIEW

STATE OF OHIO
OFFICE OF VITAL STATISTICS

CERTIFICATION OF BIRTH

STATE FILE NUMBER	1967-459002	DATE RECORD FILED	MARCH 6, 1967
NAME	JOHN ROSKA		
DATE OF BIRTH	MARCH 5, 1967	SEX	MALE
			TWIN
BIRTHPLACE	OHIO		
MOTHER"S NAME	SHIRLEY ROSKA	FATHER'S NAME	PETER ROSKA
MAIDEN NAME	TEMPLE		
MOTHER'S BIRTHPLACE	MICHIGAN	FATHER'S BIRTHPLACE	OHIO

Note: LEGAL NAME CHANGE ON FILE or BIRTH AFFIDAVIT ON FILE CORRECTING [Filed Flagged Fields from Birth Affidavit] or Delayed Birth Record: File date is correct.

This is a true certification of the name and birth facts as recorded in the Office of Vital Statistics, Columbus, Ohio. Witness my signature and seal of the Department of Health this [Date] <format DD/MM/YYYY for date printed>

State Registrar of Vital Statistics

DETACH AT PERFORATION

VERIFY PRESENCE OF DOH WATERMARK   HOLD TO LIGHT TO VIEW

STATE OF OHIO
OFFICE OF VITAL STATISTICS

CERTIFICATION OF BIRTH

STATE FILE NUMBER	1967-459003	DATE RECORD FILED	MARCH 6, 1967
NAME	DANIELLE ROSKA		
DATE OF BIRTH	MARCH 5, 1967	SEX	FEMALE
			TWIN
BIRTHPLACE	OHIO		
MOTHER"S NAME	SHIRLEY ROSKA	FATHER'S NAME	PETER ROSKA
MAIDEN NAME	TEMPLE		
MOTHER'S BIRTHPLACE	MICHIGAN	FATHER'S BIRTHPLACE	OHIO

Note: LEGAL NAME CHANGE ON FILE or BIRTH AFFIDAVIT ON FILE CORRECTING [Filed Flagged Fields from Birth Affidavit] or Delayed Birth Record: File date is correct.

This is a true certification of the name and birth facts as recorded in the Office of Vital Statistics, Columbus, Ohio. Witness my signature and seal of the Department of Health this [Date] <format DD/MM/YYYY for date printed>

State Registrar of Vital Statistics

APPENDIX DD
3701-04-1003

OHIO DEPARTMENT OF HEALTH

Reg. Dist. No. _____ 704

Primary Reg. Dist. No. _____ 839

State File No. _____

Registrar's No. _____ 299

CERTIFICATE OF DEATH

Department of Commerce — Bureau of the Census

572

1. PLACE OF DEATH:

(a) County _____ Cuyahoga

(b) _____ Cleveland (City, Village, Township)

(c) Name of hospital or institution:

Fairview General Hospital

(if not in hospital or institution, write street No. or location)

(d) Length of stay: In hospital or institution _____ 3 Days

In this community _____ 46-5-11 (Years, months or days)

2. USUAL RESIDENCE OF DECEASED:

(a) State _____ Ohio (b) County _____ Cuyahoga

(c) City or village _____ Cleveland (if outside city or village, write RURAL)

(d) Street No. _____ Harmon & Park Avenues (or RFD, give location)

(e) If foreign born, how long in U. S. A.? _____ years.

FULL

3. NAME _____ Peter Roska

(a) If veteran, _____ (b) Social Security No. _____ X

name war _____ Korean

5. Color or race _____ white

6. (a) Single, widowed, married, divorced _____ married

6. (b) Name of husband or wife _____

6. (c) Age of husband or wife if

4. Sex _____ Male

MEDICAL CERTIFICATION

20. Date of death: Month _____ January _____ day _____ 30

year _____ 1968 _____ hour _____ 10 _____ minute _____ 40 PM

21. I hereby certify that I attended the deceased from

_____ Jan. 28 _____ 19 68 _____ to _____ Jan. 30 _____ 19 68,

that I last saw h.... alive on _____ Jan. 30 _____ 19 68,

and that death occurred on the date and hour stated above. Duration

The Knott's Berry Farm Wedding Chapel

Certificate of Marriage

This is to Certify that on the *Twenty Third* day of *November*

in the year of our Lord 1968

Shirley Roska and Daniel Masden

were by me united in MARRIAGE

according to the laws of the State of California

WITNESSES

OFFICIATING MINISTER

OHIO DEPARTMENT OF HEALTH
DIVISION OF VITAL STATISTICS
CERTIFICATE OF LIVE BIRTH

177

OHIO DEPARTMENT OF HEALTH
DIVISION OF VITAL STATISTICS
CERTIFICATE OF LIVE BIRTH

CHILD—NAME Katy Danel MASDEN
DATE OF BIRTH November 18, 1975
SEX female single COUNTY OF BIRTH Cuyahoga
CITY, VILLAGE, OR LOCATION OF BIRTH Cleveland yes Fairview General Hospital
MOTHER—MAIDEN NAME Shirley Jane Temple 39 Michigan
Ohio Cuyahoga Rocky River yes 22464 Sunny Hill Road
FATHER—NAME Daniel Edwin Masden 35 Ohio
INFORMANT'S NAME OR SIGNATURE Shirley Masden mother
CERTIFIER—NAME Nov. 19, 1975 M.D. A4126
REGISTRAR—SIGNATURE John R. Sanders, M.D. 20800 Westgate #314, Fairview Park, Ohio
NOV 21 1975

CONFIDENTIAL INFORMATION FOR MEDICAL AND HEALTH USE ONLY

OHIO DEPARTMENT OF HEALTH
DIVISION OF VITAL STATISTICS
CERTIFICATE OF LIVE BIRTH

CHILD—NAME Daniel Edwin MASDEN
DATE OF BIRTH March 31, 1978
SEX male single COUNTY OF BIRTH Cuyahoga
CITY, VILLAGE, OR LOCATION OF BIRTH Cleveland yes Fairview General Hospital
MOTHER—MAIDEN NAME Shirley Jane Temple 42 Michigan
Ohio Cuyahoga Lakewood yes 4892 Madison Ave.
FATHER—NAME Daniel Edwin Masden 39 Ohio
INFORMANT'S NAME OR SIGNATURE Shirley Masden mother
CERTIFIER—NAME April 2, 1978 M.D. A4126
REGISTRAR—SIGNATURE John R. Sanders, M.D. 20800 Westgate #314, Fairview Park, Ohio
April 2, 1978

178

CELESTIAL OIL

1.

In California and Geneva, Switzerland, ravens have been observed taking nuts into their beaks, flying up to 60 feet or higher into the air and dropping them to the ground in order to crack the shells and eat the nutmeat inside. Having found a more reliable method for the less breakable walnut casings, their crow relatives have recently been witnessed in Japan carefully placing the nuts in crosswalks directly in front of lines of waiting automobiles that, when the stoplight turns green, crush the nuts under their wheels as they pass over. The birds bounce back, returning, crossing the path seemingly casually with other pedestrians, to collect their earnings.

I was recently reading a book about the lives of birds, which notes the apocryphal death of Aeschylus from a fractured skull by a tortoise shell dropped from an eagle in an effort to open the casing on the rocks to eat the flesh. I imagine Aeschylus walking on the shore, out in the open, permanently away from civilization, having relieved himself, as much as he possibly could know, of his foretold fate of being crushed by a collapsing home. Aeschylus should have known a hero cannot outrun a sealed destiny, for he always returns to his place of origin.

I had taken account of the office times listed for the *Bureau des objets coloniaux de la Renaissance et de l'empire Moghols* at the Bibliothèque Nationale and went some minutes in advance to make sure I'd encounter some one. I was patiently waiting for some one to arrive, holding the small text on the lives of birds in one hand and knocking on the various doors with the other. They were all empty despite their hours suggesting otherwise. I would have to return again.

I am not sure why I must pursue the origins of the key, but I feel connected to it. There is something in me that knows Hein will be present, that directs me toward the connection, something the viceroy meant for me or that my mother was passing on to me. I am not yet sure, but I am allowing myself to find it, to be known to it in slow time.

I entered out into the open sun and sky and walked down the Rue de Richelieu. As I set further distance between myself and the library, I thought again of the scene of Aeschylus and the eagle and of the eagles in general along the shore dropping tortoises upon the rocks, the fresh air, the mist, the crash of waves. Aeschylus did die below the shell of a tortoise, but it might be incongruous to accept such a death as his predetermined fate. The whole caricature quality of the event reminds me of *Landscape with the Fall of Icarus*, attributed with question to Bruegel the Elder, painted circa 1558. The sea is wide, open, otherwise calm, boldly colored, peppered with wave crests, ships, rocks, mountains, distant shores. This playful yet tragic canvas that I held in my imagination, while once again leaving the *Bureau des objets coloniaux de la Renaissance et de l'empire Moghols*, reminded me of a visual encounter with two other alike canvases at the Musée d'Orsay that also came to life.

When you first encounter the images, you see the white, foamy crest on the water slowly, noisily billowing like cotton candy, forming its webby curl, finally wrapping itself into the jagged, wide body of the wave that created it. The air has a suffocating salty thickness with the sun beating in a layer of moisture that suspends itself in vapors, making the objects in the distance dance around as though reflected in a fun house mirror. Little black specks with flailing limbs splash around in the water, indistinguishable from one another as seen from the shore. The thick heat from the sun gives everything an extra layer, even the silhouettes of bodies. Yet dimensions collapse in on themselves so that the horizon blends equally with the shoreline, the dark cliffs, the children building sand castles and the women sitting with parasols just a few feet away.

Standing there in the Musée d'Orsay as I was, pro-
jecting other memories simultaneously into Monet's
Grosse Mer à Etretat and Boudin's *Trouville, Scène de
plage*, and *Plage de Trouville*, and I began to wonder
how these images form, how they are collected from
the variety of senses and how I could hate something
everyone finds so pleasing. As I child I was somehow
guilt-ridden with my dislike of the seaside, only years
later realizing that it was OK for me to feel differently
from the others but also that I only disliked the over-
populated destination beaches of southern California
and other places as in the South of France. I wondered
how Monet came to paint his own *Plage de Trouville*,
getting actual grains of sand into the canvas—bringing tactile senses directly into the image, bringing the
world into the very ekphrasis of the image.

Strangely, that painting is not in the d'Orsay like the others but in London at the National Gallery. I saw it that heavy summer day when I ran from Alexandra Palace to the National Gallery, myself covered in dirty, sticky dust from the roads, from my body, from the London air. My own salted skin like the stretched, coarse canvas, like the very sand in the image and of the image made from tubes of pigment and oil, made of pigment and water and oil.

It was a week after I returned from Mongolia that I had run ten miles in the blistering London summer sun to the National Gallery to look at the pictures, trying to outrun myself to outrun my thoughts my space an ever-gnawing abyss inside outrun the story of the man with the watch. Looking with real, living eyes for the first time at Cézanne's *Bathers* and the Caspar David Friedrichs. Standing there still in my running clothes, salt covering my face and neck. Dirty running shoes covered inside and out in caramel Mongolian sand.

Every day I had run straight up mountains in the hot Mongolian sun after hours of labor in the fields with the children. The nearest town was a speck in the distance seen from the highest plateau, called Shuvu-un, Mongolian for *bird*. It had a disused gas pump, two small structures, perhaps for dumplings and tea, and a bus stop.

I saw bands of horses running across the plains. Herds of cattle and yaks being led by young boys through the mountains. Alone I watched sunsets that grew long and slow across the dusty sky, a horizon of mountain silhouettes. I dreamt I found the end of the rainbow and woke the next morning to see a circular rainbow around the sun. It's burned in my mind.

La plage, I muttered aloud as I stood there in the National Gallery, in a near whisper as if in a Hitchcock film, and was instantly startled by the sound of my own voice, transporting me back into the moment. A feeling arose as though some one else was speaking through me, while I stood there in a manner that made my being alone become acutely perceptible. I laughed, startled from hearing my own voice, there, in that space, and then the laugh itself a new startle. I wandered though the collection and soon found myself gazing at my im-age like a foreign figure through a mirror – perhaps it was intended, that mirror that reflected the new art the new aesthetic the new beauty each time, projected into it. That hanging mirror is another, more peculiar, work of art on another floor in the same gallery. I stood before it watching its inner image, this conceptual work, *Untitled Painting* by Art & Language in 1965, that has moved beyond its initial provocation and is now imbued in everything we do or think.

I wandered back to *La plage de Trouville*, the setting sun, setting low wide endless long, stretching out its arms around the sea, the horizon enveloping the sea coming together, the line strong and transparent dissolving between two. I could imagine hearing Hugo, *Quand la mer veut, elle est gaie.* When the sea desires, it is happy. And when the sea and the sky merge, blurred line between, horizonless, endless, dimensions collapsed, Rimbaud says, *C'est la mer allée / avec le soleil.* I felt myself diving headlong into an open space, the room expanding, sucking out the air and filling with the explosive inverted reverberation of a turning wave as it breaks, singing to myself, *sea, swallow me.*

Moments later, transfixed by *Untitled Painting*, my feet were cemented to the floor like pillars stationed six inches apart, facing directly forward. I felt myself holding the body erect, still, alert. I looked down. I was a foreign thing. I had consciously to tell my dirty shoes to lift to move to detach and they did. I was only slowly able to extract myself and lumber along the enormous white space of the gallery, like swimming, like dancing in a dream, hardly able to perform the function. Slow,

clumsy, hindered by nothing physically but the somehow impenetrable thick air. It took an extraordinary
effort to escape, and yet I was calm, expecting, not panicked. The end of a summer day.

Sometimes when I look at myself that way at home,
dead, still vacant in front of a mirror, I think it is always
a bad idea. It is as though I am melting, sliding off the
frame, the bones of my body. My features getting old
and worn before my eyes. There in the gallery it was
something different though. I was alive, and full. I was
reflected as I was meant to be – dirty, sweaty, exhausted,
vigorous, alone, with the whole world around me with
some perceptible change since returning from Mongolia, since the dreams began. The nuances of such a moment – being in a public space, before such a bluntly
intense work of art – create that unimaginable space
where everything is linked in a painfully inextricable
and indefinable web of still moving grey skies hanging
low over construction cranes, irregular blocks of high
rise apartments, birds that have traveled thousands of
miles through forests over oceans swooping in and out
of urban spaces landing on wires on water on branches
on soft, wet sand on droplets of starry rainbows in the
eyes of newborn children.

The world that holds that day in the National Gallery just after Mongolia feels long passed. I can still
sense it though, but it is cool, empty, finally covered
over with the smooth textures and gentle caresses of
glistening wrists and strands of auburn locks warmed
by the dark wetness of my mouth. Sometimes despite

ourselves, we stand against that past with coolness, or the past stands against us. It can no longer call out with its slippery and groping, achy tentacles but reposes far down a dark corridor, slumbering heavily, a great illness finally brought down by the slow, impossible breath of time.

I was on to Paris. I watched the world from the top of a tower in the neighborhood of Passy before moving across town a year later where I now reside. The round room at Passy was on the 8th floor, 22 meters squared, overlooking the Seine and the Eiffel Tower. Each night the lights from the *Bateaux mouches* cast their blue and orange and pink and silver lights through the 180° curve of multiple floor length windows, filtered among the curves of the iron gratings and on to the walls creating a carrousel of lights, circling the room slow and fast, beginning strong and stark, bending and swirling until each band of light suddenly vanished one by one, just as strong and stark. The elevated metro train passed four stories below the window every ten minutes, rattling the air with the impact of metal and rubber wheels smacking against the steel rods of the track, the green and white square carriages rocking back and forth, hitting one another, coarsely lulling the passengers inside.

2.

In the cemetery a few blocks away from the old apartment at Passy rests the Marquise de Talleyrand Périgord, Duchesse de Sagan, daughter of Jay Gould. She spent most of her life in Paris, married first to a swindling comte in Manhattan, having five children with him, then successfully blocking his attempt to have the marriage annulled after their divorce. The marquise then married her husband's cousin in 1908, bearing him three children and outliving him by nearly thirty years. Hélie de Talleyrand-Périgord, French duke, prince and second husband to the duchess, was the son of Boson de Talleyrand-Périgord, himself prince of Sagan, duke of Talleyrand, also cavalry officer and fantastic dandy who inspired the creation of the Duc de Guermantes and the Baron de Charlus in *A la recherche du temps perdu* with his large and graceful presence paired with his sufficiently aged, and hence somewhat senseless, state of mind. The marquise, or duchesse, spent her time mostly without her husband, residing at the seaside in Trouville at their Villa Persane and has her own literary presence as well. We might find Proust's descriptions in *A l'ombre des jeunes filles en fleurs* of the Princesse de Luxembourg resembling her, maiden name Jeanne Seillière, walking along the seaboard accompanied by a *page nègre*, a Negro page dressed in red satin.

For Easter we took a trip to Honfleur. We rented a car having been told the train stops in Deauville and

Trouville, but one must take the bus to continue up to Honfleur. We were not adverse to taking the bus, but since we were making the trip all in one day from Paris, it would not have been possible to catch it with enough time to travel by train to connect at the Deauville-Trouville station. One might suspect it would have made more sense just to visit Deauville or Trouville on a day trip from Paris, but it was because Honfleur is not connected by major transport that we considered it to be a more desirable destination, hopefully having fewer visitors passing away the breezy yet sunny Sunday. I can't say if we were wrong or not, as we visited neither Deauville nor Trouville, but Honfleur itself was overflowing with pedestrians and cars, heavy traffic and lengthy waits for the café toilets. The town was charming and beautiful, lying on the seafront, its medieval center still intact, intricate facades of half-timber and chalky limestone, Gothic and Renaissance styles, vivid colors of red, green, orange, blue, silver white, dark grey, exposed hearty beams and supports, fish scale shingles covering the entire fronts of homes, small windows peaking through.

The center square is divided by a very small harbor, called the *Vieux bassin*, where at one end the main street runs parallel with the water, and at the other end stands the 14th century church of St. Etienne, now the maritime museum. At the far end of the town is the rustic and majestic Eglise Sainte-Catherine, the largest church in France made of wood. The church was constructed after the Hundred Years War, built by navalmen axe masters and so resembling an inverted hull in appearance and containing no saw-cuts but only those cuts of the axe, as is the centuries-long tradition from the Vikings to the Normans.

In the nearby town of Caen are several more medieval churches, which appear as Proust describes the narrator's journey by car to the fictitious town of Martinville, detailing their coming into and going out of view along the way, sometimes hidden by the hills, illuminated by the sun, lost as the car curls around a turn and returning like living creatures making their presence felt. Space condenses and expands rapidly and unexpectedly, as the spires of the churches seem so very far away from the speeding automobile, *qui n'étaient plus que comme trois fleurs peintes sur le ciel au-dessus de la ligne basse des champs.* They were nothing more than three flowers painted upon the sky above the low line of fields.

Of the four churches at Caen, two are former abbeys: L'Eglise de la Sainte-Trinité for women and L'Eglise Saint-Étienne-le-Vieux for men, and all at once the same grand steeples *nous dèposa leurs pieds; et ils s'étaient jetés si rudement au-devant d'elle, qu'on n'eut que le temps d'arréter pour ne pas se heurter au porche.* They set themselves before us, and they were thrown so harshly in front of our car that we had no time to stop in order not to avoid colliding with their very doorways.

Up the coast nearby, L'Eglise Saint-Étienne in Honfleur bears a plaque dated 1899 commemorating the departure of Samuel de Champlain for North America, where he founded Quebec City in 1608. A great explorer, Champlain is considered the first European to have unveiled the Great Lakes for Europeans and to have devoted his life to the development of New France. He documented his work through the publication of detailed maps and personal accounts of his dealings with the natives. During an exhibition in 1609, which first resulted in the discovery and mapping of Lake Champlain, Champlain's group engaged in battle with 200 Iroquois, leaving their three chiefs dead, killed on sight, and permanently souring relations between the two groups.

3.

The father of Anna Gould, the Marquise de Tall-eyrand and Duchesse de Sagan, Jay Gould, self-made millionaire and railroad pioneer, befriended the aristocratic immigrant Lord Gordon-Gordon in 1873 in an effort to take control of the Erie Railroad, bribing the lord with a grant of one million dollars in stock. The lord, himself an imposter who had fled Britain after having been discovered, immediately cashed in the stock and abandoned the agreement with Gould, who had entrusted Lord Gordon-Gordon with securing the support of supposed European shareholders in the railroad that Gould was trying to control. It was a swindle on both ends start to finish, but it was Gould who lost out: although Gordon-Gordon was arrested, he fled to Canada while awaiting trial, and, as the Canadians were charmed, they disbelieved the charges and gave him extradition protection.

Appalled, Gould and several up-and-coming politicians crossed the border and kidnapped the royal imposter but were themselves arrested at the Canada line. An international incident nearly ensued when Minnesota threatened military action if Canada did not release the prisoners. After a tense but short-lived stand off, Canada relented. Gordon-Gordon thought himself safe in the northern lands, but news eventually researched Britain and the jewelers he had swindled prior to immigrating to America. A year later he was sentenced to deportation to be tried for the crimes back in his native land. The night before his deportation, Gordon-Gordon threw a party, donning expensive gifts on all his guests, and as the night hours passed and the guests said their farewells, Gordon-Gordon eventually prepared himself for his journey. With dawn approaching on the morning of August 1, 1874, Lord Gordon-Gordon put a pistol to his head and pulled the trigger.

Ninth richest man in American history, Jay Gould used his time and business skills looking for friends from the east to west coast. He got that way through friendships he made and unmade according to the greater value between the friendship itself and what might present itself as an alternative at the time. The Panic of 1857 allowed Gould to cash in on one of his greatest friendships. Charles Leupp was Gould's partner in the leather and tanning business, but when the Panic hit, Leupp lost all his investments, including his stake in the Gouldboro settlement, which Gould himself quickly bought up at a very cheap price. The friendship was demolished, the money exchanged, but the damage not yet over. Leupp's brother-in-law forcefully took over Gouldboro with arms, and eventually Gould was made to sell his share back to the family.

The Panic of 1857 had wide-reaching consequences. A great fall in the value of land in the western United States led to the Panic of 1857, where bankers in the east became wary of lending to a west that was losing its value. As a consequence, suddenly the railroads themselves too were losing their value, and all of the investments therein by the east were threatened. Many railroad companies shut down or declared bankruptcy. The public was getting nervous of the domino effect, and a subsequent series of events brought the frightening major devaluation of the railroad companies to the public's eye. The increased tension was a leading cause of the Civil War, most significantly was the impact of the Ohio Life Insurance and Trust Company, which failed due to fraudulent activity from within, and finally, the denial of Dred Scott's lawsuit for freedom from slavery broke the camel's back.

The Supreme Court's decision to dismiss Scott's case to buy his freedom based on the grounds that, as an African American, he could not be permitted to sue was a decision that raised the issue of the position towards slavery that the western territories would take. Scott himself had been living in free states though was born a slave in Virginia, and so the Scott decision opened the way for slavery in the territories, even in those in which the majority opposed it. Suddenly, everything was at stake, and civil war was imminent.

Judge Roy Bean worked as an embargo runner in Texas for the Confederacy during the Civil War. He had begun his life in Kentucky, had various exploits in California including goods trader, bullwhacker, murderer and jailbreaker. He subsequently became a barkeep, fleeing his criminal past, setting up a saloon with his brother in New Mexico, eventually moving to San Antonio where he ran a blockade of cotton in exchange for goods to the British ships supporting the South. He then tried his hand as teamster, logger, dairy farmer and butcher. At 41 he married his Mexican teen bride Virginia, had four children, left them in San Antonio and opened a saloon in the lawless area near the Pecos River, which he named Vinegaroon and where he was appointed Justice of the Peace in 1882. Calling himself the *Law West of the Pecos*, Bean ran his court out of his saloon. With the advancement of the transcontinental railroad, he moved west to an area soon to be called Langtry, which Bean falsely claimed to have named after the untouchable source of his affections, the beautiful starlet and socialite Lilly Langtry.

Bean briefly forced a meeting with Jay Gould in 1890 when he signaled Gould's train to make an emergency stop at Langtry despite the actual lack of emergency. It is said that the pair consequently shared a two-hour drink. The abrupt and unexpected halting of the train, thought to have been a blinding crash in which Gould was killed, briefly disrupted the New York Stock Exchange.

The belle of Jersey among the Channel Islands, Lilly Langtry was born in America in 1853 but only became a citizen in 1897 while living in California. She spent her childhood in the Channel Islands, where her father was the Dean of Jersey. She married at age 20 and moved to London, beginning a winding string of love affairs and relocations. After sitting for an extraordinarily flattering portrait for English painter Frank Miles, her reputation exploded on to the upper class London social scene, and she became an instant sensation. Considered exceptionally beautiful, Langtry began staring in stage productions, her inexhaustible image desired whether by photograph or painting.

Witty, intelligent and friends with Oscar Wilde, Langtry was hated by critics and loved by the public. Her life is a patchwork of marriages and affairs, including mistress to the Prince of Wales, Prince Louis of Battenberg and various American millionaires. A life as colorful as Bean's, Langtry also tried her hand in wine, horseracing, and world's first celebrity endorser, paradoxically always remaining in financial straits. Langtry spent the end of her life in Monaco where she died aged 75, having raised one child whose father has never been confirmed.

The real fear of Gould's death in 1890 by railway accident may have been inspired by Langtry's actual catastrophe when, in 1888, her entire carriage of race horses plummeted off a cliff on the way to an event in Chicago and perished, all but one, St. Saviour.

4.

My mother loved Lilly Langtry, so much so that when she and my father got together, they had a shotgun-style wedding at Knott's Berry Farm, where a false Judge Roy Bean married patrons in a recreated Jersey Lilly Saloon. My folks had never really married though. My mother had already had her fill of a life with a man, having seven children and watching him die a young, quick death. It was common knowledge that my mother never married my father, and so that made the three of us between them bastards. It was an awful term in my mind, though we were taught to believe that it was old fashioned to care.

When I was ten my mother flew out to Texas, and after some mysterious arrangements, where I felt she was transformed into the Jersey native herself, she drove back to California in an old white pick-up truck with a blue stripe along the side that she'd bought out there second hand. The truck too was some part of the mysterious transformation. Where had it come from and why? She hadn't consulted us on it; it was an emblem of what was to come, which at the time felt fresh and exciting but would turn destabilizing and impossible.

Disappearing to Texas only to turn up several weeks later in her new, used blue truck, my mom appeared brighter and ambitious, full of intangible Langtry magic. The Narnian wardrobe seemed to open inviting us all to step through fantastically and paradoxically remaining shrouded in a supernatural darkness that, as in a fairytale way, could never be penetrated. It instead enveloped me, laying a thin layer of invisible pixie dust on my eyes so that the world around me felt soft and sweet but also hidden and darkly, frighteningly mysterious.

There was a lot of excitement and commotion over mom's trip to Texas and new arrangements when she returned. She started to work on opening up her own bar in our small town in the style of Langtry, an old fashioned saloon. Everything had a Langtry touch— the meaning of which I did not at all understand but felt its enchanting dark beauty. The history of Judge Roy Bean and Lilly Langtry became an enormous and powerful myth, something I conceded I would never understand, but I could watch my mother in awe and think both of the things she knew about the history and the story and, more breathtakingly, what she—or anyone—didn't know, what couldn't be known because it was the base of the mystery itself.

The bar never opened. Despite being completely ready to go, down to the billiard tables, the five-flavor soda gun, the alcohol stock, the red vinyl booths, the latticework partitions, the used restaurant appliances in the kitchen with pots and pans large enough to cook for an army, my mother could never get the right licenses or pass some certain codes or complete some financial paperwork or whatever it may have been. It sat there empty, quietly becoming dusted, remaining perpetually in the dark with small diamonds of sunlight shining through the lattice in the morning.

With the restaurant and bar empty and dark day after summer day, the three of us bastard kids used to play card games like Blackjack, 31 and Rummy sitting on barstools drinking sodas from the gun. It had a flavor different from soda in a bottle and made us feel like we were real bar patrons. We watched it shoot out of the gun, thick and foamy, each flavor connected with two small hoses hidden inside the large hose that went under the sink, one hose to the carbonated soda water and the other to the distinguishing flavor syrup. We'd go outside on the patio and smoke from straws in the cool air.

There are no railroads in my hometown. It sits high in the mountains accessible only by three skinny and windy roads coming up from the Los Angeles basin. It was first inhabited by Native Americans for thousands of years until the white man arrived on horseback in the 19th Century when gold was discovered, traveling two days by carriage to reach it from the flatlands below. They hired Chinese laborers to build a railroad to the mountain valley at 7,000 ft., but it was abandoned once automobiles were introduced, a journey which now takes one hour. Langtry's time in California was nowhere near our town, though in a geographically similar environment on Clear Lake north of San Francisco. Bean too lived in California about fifty years before Langtry—San Diego's first mayor.

5.

In *The Octopus* Frank Norris writes of the clash between the California wheat growers and the monopolistic corruption of the expanding railroad. Six months before Judge Roy Bean's death at age 78 after a drinking binge, came Norris' death, not by drink but unexpected appendicitis at age 32. Based on the Mussel Slough affair, *The Octopus* is concerned with the destructive and underhanded ways of both parties, the farmers and the railroad, as they each seek to undermine the other in a dishonest property exchange. The rivalry ended in a fatal shootout, where both sides, as well as the peace-keepers themselves, lost lives.

Having left Chicago as a youth to study painting in Paris, Norris went on to attend Berkeley before moving to San Francisco and becoming a journalist and naturalist writer, taking great influence from Emile Zola. He attempted to write with a voice of actual experience and observation. A correspondent first in South Africa and later Cuba during the Spanish-American war, Norris was a socialist who focused on suffering and inequality in his fiction, often highlighting the ambiguity of good and bad, presenting the corruption of both sides, which have been equally harmed as they have done harm. The legacy of his reputation is tarnished by his frequent Antisemitic angle, randomly selecting Jewish figures as villains, such as in the unfinished trilogy *The Epic of the Wheat*, where the railway company representative, S. Behrman, is demonized as a money-grubbing scoundrel.

It is hard to allow public figures, as we know them, to have real personalities. We do not forgive what we perceive to be their human flaws. It would undermine what they represent to us. Norris himself felt that the novelist must *possess a sense of his responsibilities*. I am convinced he would be surprised to find himself remembered significantly as an Anti-semite, it normally being problematic to use current political perspectives on historical moments. Norris' Anti-semitism was not radical during his time, as his ideas were common—a great problem itself, a problem too for hindsight analysis.

Norris is an example of how we make sense of relating the literary text both to a social dynamic and to the author. We look at how the text functions internally, taking it as a solitary object, like an unaffected world self-contained, and then again in relation to how it affects us. Deleuze and Guattari remind us to avoid judging literature politically in the way we are prone to mistake the relation between the text and the social context. What can writing do, particularly novels? I wonder if Norris's work then is either, or at all, a critique on the socialism of the content, or on the personality and beliefs of the author.

The relation between the literary object and the world is complicated, an idea lending itself to Norris' own theory that any given age uses one form of art over another to best express itself. I find, though, that it's too reductive a picture to promote, and want to say that instead of agreeing or disagreeing that the current age is music, as Norris wanted to prophesy, we might say it's something more akin to being a new, blurred space that exists between writing and reality, writing truth and fiction, writing for an audience and for oneself. Most prominently, we write out in public now, electronically and across the world instantaneously. We have moved away from the possibility, I think, of believing in any form to express, in any real or concrete or *truthful* way, the reality from which such expression comes, and so we turn toward the multiplicity of truth and of form that is blended in the writerly expression once considered wholly private, as in diaries, and personal, as in autobiographies. We delight in what we currently perceive as the real, but we also love the complexity of knowing none of it could ever be the real that it claims to be. It's always too much and never enough.

Dying six months before Frank Norris, Samuel Butler may have had some of these ideas in mind when he wrote *Erewhon* in 1872, satirizing the concept of utopia or, rather, the attempted implementation of utopian values in contemporary Victorian society. Butler was interested in evolutionary thought and wrote about the application of Darwinian selection both in terms of intellectual development and in the possibility of machines developing consciousness and evolving on their own.

In *Différence et repetition*, written in 1968, Deleuze borrows from Butler's language and ideas, using 'erewhon' itself to mark the concept of *nulle part*, nowhere, and of *l'ici-maintenant*, the here-and-now. It is both too much and never enough, both ideal, nonexistent, and actual, mundane. English translators can take advantage of the play on words, where 'no-where' becomes 'now-here'. Deleuze himself plays from English to French, explaining the concept of *on*, 'we' or 'one', is also contained in the *erewhon*. How we define our concepts shifts and moves nomadically, Deleuze contends. They are not static but constantly in flux, gazing back upon something in order to stabilize that flux or multiplicity itself. This task is in the nature of philosophy and is the paradoxical history of philosophy: a perpetual pursuit to continue the path forged by disintegrating the present in order to confirm or define that same present. Calling upon Nietzsche, Deleuze names this necessary quality *intempestive*, untimely, because it is always necessarily outside of itself, opening paths and routes for future untimely meditations.

Later in 1972 in *L'Anti-oedipe* with Guattari, the pair further draws on Butler in order to develop their theory of *la machine du désir*, the desiring-machine. Why machines? Because they are composites, and it is impossible to break down the production of its total sum into just one element. It is the collective force. A central subject in Butler's satire states how the people of Erewhon live without machines because of their mistrust that the machines could, in a natural, Darwinian evolutionary step, develop consciousness and take over. Is it a founded fear? Deleuze and Guattari explain, it seems, that machines are limbs and organs that are subsumed by bodies-without-organs. What is a body-without-organs? Individuals are not static, lacking things but are *les corps-sans-organs*, bodies-without-organs: they are, we are, open horizons for fulfillment, undifferentiated realms below our appearances, a proto-world without definition or core. In presenting the fear of machines in the Erewhonians, Deleuze and Guattari believe that Butler is denouncing an underlying sense of unity to the machine, rejecting the archaic concept of vitalism and asserting that all beings are actually components to be taken, used, joined and connected, modified, one from another, here to there, all across the collective *plan d'immanence*, plane of immanence.

Desire produces reality. It adds it up across all forms. In opposition to Freud, Deleuze and Guattari assert that desire is not lack but production. Freudian theory produces a self that begins its conscious life by perpetually seeking to make up for a lack that has been removed at the infant level (the loss of the mother, the detection of the lack of penis, etc.). Yet this analysis undermines itself by proposing a normalized basis from which to begin and from which to judge and analyze the lack in desire. Much of the 20th Century accepted that this basis was nothing but Freud's own personal sense of normal. Deleuze was not so sure that could be permitted any longer.

Deleuze shows us that when we deconstruct language, and our use of it, we see that there is not a stable or pure self either hiding its true nature from itself (and constantly trying to make up for it) or wholly and negatively affected by a sense of lack that it must recuperate its life long. (As Wittgenstein reminds us, it is within our usage of language and the rules of the game that define it that sense is made. Its misuse creates metaphysics.) There is no incomplete subject in need of fulfillment. Human desires, the will to pursue, to attain, our needs and wants are elements of the desiring-machine creating and ejecting desire into the world. Desire is flowing everywhere, creating, producing, going in and out. Desire is not lack but constant production. There is a universe of virtual desire, a plane of immanence, that is full of all the possibilities from which to create, extract and build desire. It is the collective self.

The depth of what we imagine ourselves to be, the bodies-without-organs, is but the potential to be many possibilities, shooting in all directions to the limitless limit, connecting to other bodies-without-organs, creating new *lignes de fuite*, lines of flight, on the plane of immanence. We run, escape, play through avenues that themselves produce new desires and new avenues.

The body-without-organs is a horizon and not a goal because it is perpetual. A machine is the force of production, and so the desiring-machine is the force of the production of desire in all of the ways in which it can be manifest, through the body-without-organs, through itself, through moving and reconnecting, nomad-traveling, any kind of trajectory that we can imagine when we imagine desire. Deleuze says, *Nous croyons à un monde où les individuations sont impersonelles, et les singularités, pré-individuelles: la splendeur du 'ON'*. We believe in a world where individuations are impersonal, and singularities are pre-individual: the splendor of '*on*'.

The '*on*' —this 'we'— is the collective self, like Black Elk and his expression of the collective as given to him by the Grandfathers. We are the singularity through transcending the sense of the singular. Whitman, Hein, the victims of the Haymarket Affair, the snake and the lily, the birds of Simorgh, *Erinnerung* and *Gedächtnis*: how we give our sense of identity and understanding over to a collectivity to help and define us —the 'us', the '*on*', that is not many, but one that is many.

6.

I decided to walk back to the Bibliothèque Nationale hoping once again to speak to some one about the case of ancient keys. I was not sure what I was looking for anymore, if it is something that will explain the story of the man with the watch or the appearance of the viceroy and enchantress. Still, I am drawn to it as though its origin is connected to my future.

The walk from my place to the library takes about an hour, passing through many different neighborhoods on the way. The city is in constant flux with traffic and noise, and the air is always unsettled. Pedestrians cross at every corner, angle, direction without hesitation without looking without right. Cars are honking horns, swerving, cursing, gesticulating, taxis dropping off passengers picking up others, businessmen and tourists hailing them unsuccessfully twenty paces into the road. Hairdressers are beating old rugs against the trees along the boulevard, smoky steam rises up from the hot plate of the crepe vendors, the eyes of patrons look blank around as they drink dirty espressos on the café tables outside, some one is pushing muddy water into the gutter in front of their shop with an aching, soggy broom. The sidewalks are littered with unnameables. Dogs are walked, cigarettes are inhaled and discarded, change is dropped into crusty plastic coffee cups placed in front of beggars with old pieces of luggage overflowing and dark, dirty clothing, grocery bags, blankets, books, mysterious objects bulging against the sides.

I arrived at the *Bureau des objets coloniaux de la Renaissance et de l'empire Moghols* again during office hours. It looked no different than on my last two visits. Just as musty, just as empty. I knocked on each door along the corridor without any response from within until the last one. Almost immediately I heard a small and distant *entrez!*

Surprised yet with a mechanical response, I opened the door cautiously and was met with a small, stuffy room cluttered with books, objects, folders, papers sticking out in all directions, a layer of dust upon everything, and golden rods of light beaming in through the sole window highlighting the gentle particles of sky as they floated through the very still space. In one corner of the small room was an old, wooden desk, darkened creases along its length, harboring the muck from years past. The desk was also covered in such a variety of papers and objects that it looked completely useless. Behind it at a man clearly in his 80s or even older, wearing a worn, grey suit jacket and beige slacks. His shirt was creased, faded, with the tips of the collar bending upward. The top of his bald head was covered in liver spots. His eyebrows were overgrown and curling down toward his watery blue eyes. His mouth hung partway open as he greeted my entrance, half-surprised half-indifferent, and I saw his rigid, yellowing teeth, and the dry, cracking edges of his lips quiver slightly. I couldn't understand why such an old man would still be working in an office.

Bonjour, monsieur. J'espère que je ne vous dérange pas.

Bonjour. Est-ce qu'il y a quelque chose avec laquelle je peux vous aider? Is there something I can help you with?

I hope I am not disturbing you. I am interested in the collection of ancient keys that I saw just outside in the hall.

And what is it that interests you?

Could you tell me more about them?

I'm afraid there isn't a lot I am able to share.

In particular, I am interested in the key that is missing, with a marker, its image, fourth from the right, the 17th Century key that…

Ah! He exclaimed, cutting me off, his face now alight. That key was recovered—.

He cut himself off.

I was a young man, he added softly, looking now toward the window.

His gaze turned inward as though taken by old memories.

Yes, well, what is its origin?

He continued staring blankly ahead for several moments and was suddenly startled back into awareness. Hmm? Oh, yes, well, you read the description?

I did.

Yes, well, I'm afraid we don't know much more than that. These kinds of things… he waved his arms carelessly and sighed with an air of exasperation but more of resignation.

I had a feeling he knew something more but could not say. I wanted to press the matter but needed to restrain myself.

Well, monsieur, where *is* the key? I see it is no longer in the display case. Has it been moved? Its description does not address its absence.

The old man's entire presence seemed to shrink and darken. Please, he said. Have a seat.

I did.

I'm afraid, he began again, that information is unavailable, he said to me in a somber and unconvincing tone.

Pardon? I asked, wondering why he asked me to sit if he had nothing to say. As the old man cleared his throat, he stared directly at me or through me, into me, for what seemed an eternity.

Unfortunately, he began, exhaling deeply, the key is not in our collection here. It belongs elsewhere. It was first displayed in the library when I was a young man. I will tell you, because—because I can see you have your own personal investment in the relic, I will tell you that this key was the reason I entered this *métier*. I spent many years—how shall I say—around that key. Indeed, it was I who—

He paused. Something was causing him to struggle. Monsieur?

Ah, well, it was I who brought the key here, but—it is not in the collection here any longer, I'm afraid.

I returned his gaze without speaking. He exhaled deeply.

It's gone. The key has been removed.

Suddenly, his words sped up, became curt. His body closed up, and he ended abruptly.

I persisted, Was the key in the library all that time or...?

The old man seemed briefly to relax, giving over somewhat to my innocent inquisition.

It is a strange and interesting question. The truth is—and I am not sure why I need to be telling you this—but the truth is that the key is held privately, as indicated in the description. The owner had in the past loaned it to the library but has recently removed it. I cannot say why.

But, monsieur, you just told me it was you who recovered the key, n'est-ce pas?

Yes, indeed. That is true. Thank you for coming.

He stared straight at me, unflinchingly and with speaking something unspoken.

Yes, monsieur. I replied, realizing I had probably asked too many questions and thus took my cue to leave. Thank you for your time.

Yes, he said, and then quickly added, please do come again.

I looked at him in surprise. His eyes softened, looking kind, and our gazes were locked as I rose from my seat until I turned toward the door.

Merci beaucoup.

Je vous en prie. You're welcome.

7.

Out on the street, I breathed the open air deeply, suddenly feeling refreshed and a strong desire to absorb the speed and vitality of the living city. I had no idea what would come of that meeting, but I was excited and optimistic. I walked for hours down alleyways and boulevards, passing the bakeries with their intricate creations in the windows, fresh fruits jelled atop tarts, the currants still on their stems, light and creamy éclairs painted in bright, glossy frosting, giant, airy meringues with their crisp, chewy texture. I passed old brasseries with worn-looking patrons drinking thick espressos, staring absently through the endless windows, casually dropping cigarette butts on the already littered linoleum floor. I passed restaurants with brass-accented interiors and watched patrons cut overcooked steaks, stab the pommes frites with their forks, leave the creamy salads untouched. I passed the numerous banks, archaic post offices, endless boutiques, chain clothing stores, questionable electronic outlets, beggars, pedestrians, groups of suburban teenagers, gypsy children, businessmen, nannies with strollers, everyone hustling. Paris is out in storm each day.

I thought of the collective self as I navigated my body through that massive, unruly urban construct. I tried to imagine Black Elk taking part in Buffalo Bill's Wild West and how he perceived that experience through his heritage through the voices of the Grandfathers through the destruction of his people he saw and felt through his reconciliation with a world constantly changing, unknown, unexpected. I thought of Annie Oakley doing the same and wonder how she felt about being the greatest female sharpshooter and wondering if being in Buffalo Bill's Wild West show was something she was proud of and what it meant then and what it means now. I thought of Calamity Jane who is often remembered in tandem with Annie Oakley, though they were as different as two independent women could be. Calamity Jane also appeared in Buffalo Bills' show, as a storyteller beginning 1893. Her drunkenness and her far-fetched truths contributed to her dismissal before too long.

In 1903 *Wild West Magazine* published the first of many tales to come of the exploits of Calamity Jane, so named, according to Jane herself, due to her fierce fighting against the Native Americans and her extraordinary rescue of Captain Egan in Wyoming when his men fled, leaving him for dead. The accuracy of most of Jane's claims is at best highly dubious. She is known above all as a drunken fabricator of much of her gun-slinging, bull-whacking experiences as a frontiers person.

One of the first tales in *Wild West Magazine* involves Jane escaping the clutches of Black Elk and his braves. It had been said that she had terrorized them far too much to be left *any longer at liberty*, and so they came after her. Whether or not Black Elk ever encountered Calamity Jane at all is uncertain, and the same can be said for the various legendary figures Jane claimed to know, including Wild Bill Hickok, who, depending on the circumstances of the story as told by Jane, was her husband, her lover, her betrothed, her hero and she his. When she unexpectedly died on a train after a drinking binge, Jane was buried next to Hickok, whether by misunderstanding or, what is also said, as a joke against Hickok who wanted nothing to do with Jane alive or dead.

Stories of the Wild West came from the mouths of the lying perpetrators themselves but also their biographers, fans and enemies, giving them legacies matched only by Greek gods and goddesses. Hickok himself spun a tale or two, giving a rare interview to Sir Henry Morton Stanley in 1867 where he boasts of his lawless, sharpshooting human kills. At each telling, Jane and Hickok's stories became more unruly and exciting, and we now remember such characters precisely due to the caricatures they strangely created of themselves and lived out and have now posthumously become permanently.

Hickok's famed interviewer was none other than the English bastard child John Rowlands who became Sir Henry Morton Stanley, first, after voyaging to New Orleans from his native Wales at the age of 18 and asking to be adopted by a local merchant, Henry Hope Stanley; second, after returning to the United Kingdom at age 30 as a respected explorer and being knighted for his service to the British Empire in Africa. After fighting in the American Civil War both for the Union and Confederacy, Stanley established himself as an overseas correspondent for the *New York Herald*, which sent him to the Congo in 1871 to find the Scottish missionary David Livingstone, who had been missing in the region for some time. Their apocryphal exchange upon meeting became a common line of satire, *Doctor Livingstone, I presume?* Or the reference to the line has itself become the satire.

With Livingstone's rescue, Stanley's African exploits were only beginning. For the *Daily Telegraph* he headed a team to follow the dangerous and unknown Congo out to sea, the last great and treacherous mystery of exploration in Africa. All of Stanley's expeditions resulted in massive loss of life, but none could compare to the charting of the Congo where only a third of 400 remained, Stanley being the only white man left. Such a sum also attests to Stanley's personal disregard for human life and in particular the human life of natives. He was brutal in his command, and it is not uncommon to hear stories of his killing of the Africans as though they were worthless and expendable.

It is evident that Joseph Conrad used Stanley in part as one of his influences in the creation of Kurtz of *Heart of Darkness*. Two other significant figures were Georges-Antoine Klein, whom Conrad transported on his Congo steamer when he was hired by a Belgian trading company to transport ivory. Klein was an agent of the company and was meant to be picked up and returned to Europe, having fallen seriously ill at the inner most trading post deep in the African jungle. He died en route back and was buried on its banks, just like Kurtz in the novel. Second source of inspiration was Leon

Rom, Belgian solider turned chief at Stanley Falls on the Congo, who decorated his grounds with the decapitated heads of his enemies, just like Kurtz in the novel.

Conrad was Polish though born in the Ukraine under Russian rule. He became an orphan and sailor in France at a young age and eventually a citizen of England after years of efforts to be released from Russian nationality. Conrad spent nearly 20 years as a British Merchant Marine, 10 of those at sea, drawing from this period for the very personal material used for his writing. It was a decade before *Heart of Darkness* that Conrad captained the steamer up the Congo at the Belgian trading company's request to recover Klein, when the gravely ill company agent died on the return journey. Conrad himself nearly died, and that, paired with his witnessing endless atrocities of colonialism, imperialism and their many tentacles of corruption, caused Conrad to give up the sea trade altogether and become a writer, spending the rest of his life with his family in the English countryside.

Heart of Darkness explores the potentially natural cruelties deep in the core of man. Marlow the narrator tells the disturbing story of his voyage up the Congo to rescue Kurtz, while he is aboard a ship on the Thames with other seemingly good-natured and well-positioned sailors. This frame narrative reminds the reader of the contrast between the two locations and their geo-political and economic placement in the world. Africa is shrouded in darkness, in the white man's perception of its natives—it is 'The Dark Continent' to the Victorians, both composed of 'dark' peoples and reflective of the white man's mental darkness in his lack of knowledge of their landscape and cultures—and also in the mystery and obfuscation of the atrocities committed there.

Conrad is often considered a tragedian because his worldview focuses on cut-throat, Darwinian evolution and on materialism (in opposition to any kind of spiritualism), along with the revelation that the metaphysical is a creation within that material reality. In this way, the spiritual becomes nothing but a treasure, possessed and guarded by man. The world itself contains all that is. Yet for Conrad, through this observation, man is able to experience the awe of recognizing the grandeur that the material world creates. *Heart of Darkness* is replete with discontinuities, discrepancies, contradictions—Conrad's method, as professor Sandhya Shetty claims, for discouraging the belief that the world can be understood but also to encourage the discovery of this awe that the material world inspires.

As we see by the end of the novel, Marlow enters his own darkness, yet is strangely also able to transform part of that into light—thus confirming the discontinuous and contradictory nature of the world—when he chooses to remove the final barbaric line of Kurtz's report (*exterminate all the brutes*) and when he lies to Kurtz's fiancé about her beloved's dying words, replacing *The horror! The horror!* with the dear lady's name, easing her grief.

Conrad was well respected and connected and first befriended the Scottish politician and reformer Cun-

ninghame Graham when the latter offered an introduction to his publisher Edward Garnett for Conrad's
first novel. Though Cunninghame Graham was from a
prominent, conservative family, he became well known
as a socialist in his service for sweeping reformations
across the UK including establishment of the 8-hour
workday, Scottish home rule, universal suffrage, na-
tionalization of industry and land, free school meals
and a collection of other radical concepts. Prior to his
engagement in politics, Cunninghame Graham, whose
mother was a Spanish noblewoman, traveled the world,
settling for a time in South America, where he became
a wealthy cattle rancher, nicknamed Don Roberto.
He is said to have collected an impressive amount of
eclectic experiences including masquerading as a Turk-
ish sheikh in Morocco, prospecting for gold in Spain,
teaching fencing in Mexico City, befriending Buffalo
Bill in Texas and single-handedly digging his own wife's
grave.

Cunninghame Graham befriended other well-
known figures including George Bernard Shaw, William Morris and John Galsworthy. He and Conrad became correspondents in 1898, with Conrad respecting
Cunninghame Graham tremendously. Conrad had an
incredibly excellent memory, and, in his capacity to reproduce ideas, thoughts and exact words of those of
others he had digested, his works sometimes reveal
his various inspirations and influences, often in a cu-
riously exact yet wholly new manner. In the case of
Cunninghame Graham, Conrad modifies a proverb of

Archimedes in a letter to the latter in 1899 akin to Cunninghame Graham's use of it in an essay in *Commonweal* in 1890.

Cunninghame Graham writes, *Fear is a good lever too, you know. Having your lever, though you want a fulcrum...Archimedes could have moved the world could he have found a fulcrum.*

In the letter Conrad writes, *Madness and despair! Give me that for a lever and I'll move the world*—a passage that he also then quotes in his novel *The Secret Agent* of 1907.

What parallels their two uses, and distinguishes Conrad's from merely being his own modification of Archimedes', is the replacement of *lever* with, in one instance, *fear* and the other *madness and despair*. Archimedes' own claim did not hold such doubt or tragedy.

Conrad modifies the same Archimedes' proverb again in 1912, in another unusual and new way, this time speaking of mathematics.

Don't talk to me of your Archimedes' lever. He was an absentminded person with a mathematical imagination. Mathematics commands all my respect, but I have no use for engines. Give me the right word and the right accent and I will move the world.

*****

Imagination, engines, machines—I might imagine engines and machines operating on the same plane, perhaps they are the same thing. All beings are machines including engines and perhaps including imagination too, and all have the potential to expand and modify, join up limbs and bodies, reconnect, intertwine, disconnect, move about, lie still. The right word and the right accent incite us into entangling ourselves in the impossible journey toward dark abysses, the open planes of immanence, the virtual and potential lines of flight, avenues for exploring for becoming for explaining for living, filling up these bodies-without-organs. The words unravel on the page, and we come face to face with that reflection where the light does not escape as much as the light escapes. We try to unravel ourselves from the image we see. We cannot unravel ourselves from the reflection of ourselves. This is the right word and the right accent—that troubles us and entices us, that compels us, loves us and destroys us, and we live again, that causes us to experience the ecstatic surge of blood through our veins, life pulsing through, death and the undoing, connectivity, desperation and the empty moment of time standing still or speeding along raising the hair on our arms in its wake, millions of goose bumps that burn to the touch.

We are the '*on*', the collective self.

I am a 'we'.

8.

A week hadn't passed when I was surprised to find that the old man had summoned me to his home. He did not live far from the library, and so I walked there, crossing the corners of three *arrondissements* from my place to his. I climbed the four flights of stairs and heard him shuffling across a creaking wooden floor to answer the door. He was wearing the same or a similar suit to what I'd seen him wearing at his office in the library, and though I had only met him that one time, I noticed he looked markedly more aged and quite grave on this meeting. He motioned me into his modest apartment, and I saw that he had prepared a kettle of tea, which was steaming atop a small table in the center of the room.

S'il vous plaît, asseyez-vous. Please, take a seat.

Merci beaucoup, monsieur. Comment allez-vous? Thank you, sir. How are you?

I didn't quite know what to say, how to address him and was even afraid to inquire what I was doing there, feeling both excited and nervous that I already knew the answer.

Welcome to my home. I'm sure you are asking yourself why I invited you here. It is not so customary for the French to extend such an informal gesture so quickly, or, in such a case as the context for our relationship if we have one, even at all.

Yes, monsieur.

But let me be frank. I have made a profound revelation. I am aware of your interest, and it is evident to me that something greater is at work here. My involvement, I see, is to perform my service in this continuum of which I know I am a small part. Your involvement, well, only you know that, but, from the experiences I have had in my many long years, I imagine it too has a particular service, is an emblem in the greater landscape the ends of which we as these particular individuals cannot see or know, at least not from the angles with which we are provided in this here and now.

He used the word *l'ici-maintenant*.

Yes, monsieur.

I have the key, he suddenly announced.

I let out a barely audible gasp.

My father was a very private, a secretive man, you might say, though I know that larger factors were always at play that affected how he chose to guard or share information. And I as a result have adopted the same behavior. Before you had even entered my office I knew suddenly that this story was coming to an end, perhaps I should say, beginning... that is, somehow coming full circle, or in any case—

He couldn't seem to find the right words. He trailed off. I didn't know what to say, if there was anything to say. Luckily, he began again.

Would you like some tea?

Thank you.

He poured us each a wonderfully aromatic cup, and I felt the variety of herbs awaken my senses. There were several large paintings hanging about, and the walls themselves were covered in a faded but intricately patterned paper. It spanned the entire room and gave it what I imagined to be a 19th century air. Old photographs were pinned to one section of the wall in the corner near a doorway that I assumed passed into the only other room of the apartment. There was a closed door next to the front door, and this, I concluded, was the toilet. Aside from the table and two chairs, the room in which we were sitting also had a desk, near the photographs, which was covered in stacks of papers, a collection of stamps, irregularly shaped folders, aging books with broken spines and even an ink well. There was a small sofa with gently curving wooden arms at the other end, under one of two windows that looked out onto a dark passageway.

His gentle, crackling voice broke the momentary silence: I am troubled in this attempt to speak about my family in the world or of the interrelations of all, of us all, and also between us, as we are—this, as a collective swirl of humanity.

It is necessary to be more than one, you see, the old man went on. There is the noise from so many voices moving beyond the possibility of the story of one man. Though that story is still relevant, it belongs to a history of its own telling and the collection of those stories and histories and tellings. What results is an absence of the story itself and instead an unconscious submission to the body, the collective if you will, from whence it came. Ironically, with that in place, all of the original feelings of existence, of despair, of melancholy, of the beauty in the surprise of being alive, they are laid waste, set aside, their once delicate presence no longer mattering but instead serving now as the basis for something peculiarly even less meaningful that has become infinitely meaningful.

I didn't quite know if he was trying to explain something more or was just speaking to fill the room, but he visibly relaxed and took a deep breath. I began to feel as though he lost a sense of my presence at I sat there in his private quarters and that he was then speaking for the sake of the words as they lingered in space, softly cascading down past his chin, his chest, his body and into the air, floating around the room into me and around and through the cracked glass of the window into the world beyond.

Telling the story of oneself is impossible, the old man went on. No one appears to recognize this, or surely those who do have already forgotten and so try again. There is no story, you see, there is none at all. Yet strangely there is a collective spreading of moments, experiences and morsels that appear as stories so that what lies beyond us, each of us has vanished into the meaning of what is and what is to come and, in fact, what has been.

Quickly adding as though an afterthought, he concluded: We must remember to carry on. We must remember to carry it all on.

I didn't understand. He could see that.

Alas, he sighed deeply. The story is irrelevant. I suppose we are made aware and we are not. We are coming and going, you see.

Monsieur?

The old man ignored my confusion, stood up and walked toward the desk. He opened a cupboard then a small drawer and finally pulled out a small leather satchel.

I would like to give you this. Indeed, he paused, looking out into an imaginary distance, it belongs to you.

He held the satchel out to me. I slowly raised my arm, not breaking his gaze, wondering how I would accept this, knowing I could not refuse but experiencing such a rush of emotion that I thought I would be unable to contain myself. I slowly took it into my hand and quietly slid it into my pocket without a sound without looking away.

Thank you.

Indeed, he replied. I pray you will use it wisely. We are limited in fewer ways than we suspect.

I nodded, not understanding, and made no reply.

Thank you for coming, he kindly said, not retaking his seat. I knew I was then meant to leave. I stood up, shook his hand, thanked him again, my head in a blur. He opened the door for me, and as I stepped out onto the small landing before descending the stairs, he stood in his doorway for a moment and said,

It is better to keep your breath cold.

Stunned and speechless, Au revoir, I said mechanically.

Lips pursed, he nodded solemnly, graciously.

9.

I awoke the next morning with senses heightened. I imagined it would be like this. The viceroy calls me back to the table, and though I am obliged to obey, I stay that moment longer at the knees of my mother. She cups my chin and my cheeks and my face in her hands, and she looks down on me, and what she says to me what I hear without hearing, what I know, suddenly and already know: I am a 'we'.

As I tore myself out of that space and took in the breath of the air in the room around me, moving away from the scene of the table of the viceroy and the dancing enchantress and my mother there at the table, what I suddenly knew: I was bearing something more than my death in me but another's and its death. I was pregnant.

Captain January V

It's too much. I can't keep up. I can't keep it up. It's too much.

I need a drink.

It's too much. I can't keep this up. These children. It's too much. I am a horrible mother. No, stop. No. Don't. No. I am a wasted person. No, don't! I am lost. I am lost. I am marooned. Shipwrecked. Trapped. Finished.

Shirt, you're a disgrace. A disgrace—who the hell?

Who gives a damn? To hell with them. I don't care that damn, hot damn. Don't care what they think. Who? I'm going to get what I deserve. All of my children will get those benefits. I am an artist! This is— what the hell? This is nonsense. How did I end up like this? Look at me. Disgusting. What the hell? Who said anything about it? God damn it.

All of my children will get those benefits. To hell with them. No one will know the difference. It doesn't matter if they don't have the same father. Forge those damn papers. Who gives a damn. Damn. These three little ones, they're getting those damn veteran benefits too, dammit, even if their Pollack dad is not the same dad. What dad? Who the hell? Even if their daddy's my stupid brother-in-law! What have I done? Oh Peter Peter. Who the hell? What a story. What a story. They need to make a movie about me. I'm really something! What the hell.

I need a drink.

I can't keep this up. I have to get out of here. Some one needs to take care of those damn kids. I can't do it anymore. Those little—who the hell? I don't know why I had them. I'm sorry. I know. God damn it all. Damn it! It was a mistake. Oh those sweeties. Stupid Pollack. An accident! What a way to go. Those kids—they're beautiful. I don't care. Damn it all! Beauty didn't get anything anywhere! I'm finished. They'll survive. Everyone survives. Those creatures. It's my fault. It's too bad. Those little. God damn it. Doesn't matter anymore. Not my problem to solve now. They'll find a way. Everyone finds a way. Everyone's got to find a way.

I'm sorry! Little shits! I'm worn out. Those poor little bastards. What have I done? What the hell? God—.

At least they'll get the goddamn benefits. I have to get those goddamn Social Security cards sorted out. Change their names. They'll get the benefits too. Goddamn benefits.

I deserve better! What is this shit? All of my talents wasted! These people are idiots. Idiots! What the hell? Who?

Where's my drink?

If I could just get some money, you see—. If I could just get some money together I could open a restaurant. It could really make it this time! I need some damn money. I've got to call up that old guy. What's his name? Who the hell? Oh, I can see it now! Crowded and full of life. Music, the lights! Give me a goddamn break! Give me a goddamn break, some one! The smiling faces, the rich men. My Cadillac. My goddamn body. My food. They love my goddamn food. The compliments. Finally get a little respect, a little credit for my talents. Those little shits. They love my cooking. They always do.

I can't keep working this goddamn kitchen at the Moose Lodge. Those disgusting old men. Dammit! But I take it. I take their filthy bodies to bed, and get what I deserve. I take their dirty old money and walk out the door. I've got to call that old cowboy bastard. I'm going to get what I came for, and it sure isn't minimum wage. Fools. Disgusting fools. Who the hell?

I should have been an artist! I'm goddamn good enough! I could have been somebody. What the hell?

Why am I not somebody?

Why am I nobody? How does it happen like this? These goddamn years.

I should have been somebody. I'm Elizabeth Taylor. I look like Elizabeth Taylor. They always said. Look at these eyes! And my voice! I should have been a movie star. We used to sing such beautiful melodies. How the hell? How did I never make anything of it? Where's it gone? I was meant for goddamn failure? This body these memories the doors closed before I knew they existed. What the hell? You get out there, and it's been decided! There's nothing for you, Shirt. What a load of shit. No, there's nothing for you. You never had a goddamn chance, you bastard! There was never anything for you, and you goddamn know it and you goddamn knew it. Clear the day of my birth they were never marked for me. Just like that. Always just like that. What the hell? Marked for no one, goddamn it, a void out there beckoning and empty with no path to get in.

How do the bastards get through? I just need a goddamn break. I'm so tired.

Where's my drink? I need another drink.

I'm so tired. Memories. So many memories. Disgust. So much disgust. Filth. So much filth. What have I done? What the goddamn hell? So much to wipe away, to not remember. To dull, to dim. I'm a goddamn poet.

My children. Those children. The sick cycle. I can't take it anymore. I can't take it! Pathetic. A drink. A drink.

Goddamn it all. They grow too. They'll have children, goddamn it. It doesn't matter what happens. It doesn't matter if I'm here or not. It doesn't matter anything. I just have to get out of this. I need a break. I need to go. Gone. Get gone. They don't need me. I need to deaden, to find where there is nothing, nothing to think about. What? No more memories, goddamn it. To hell with it. Memories. It's all just damn memories. The shit. To shit with it! Plagued with memories of disgust.

Dammit, I need money. I just need some money. If I only had some money. Never a winning ticket. Never the slots. Oh, but once in a while, Shirt! Once in a while you win! I've just got to get the right combination. It's possible. It happens to folks. You see it on TV. They win. I can win! It'll happen to me. I'm destined. I'm meant for it. I am. My break. It's coming my way, I know it. They win. I can win! I am meant for it. All I need to do is win.

What the hell is—?

All these goddamn children. Too much to care for. No one to know me, to need me, to take it away from me. What have I done? What the hell is going on?

Goddamn bottle is already empty. I'll go over to the tavern early. That always works. Dottie lets me take what I want when I'm working, when I'm in the kitchen. Dottie's a nice girl. A bit stupid. They're always a bit stupid. Good for me. Never notice what I take home in my bag either. And I think she's been putting some kind of stash each night in the planter behind the slots. Just have to wait until she uses the toilet next time. Can't figure out yet how to make sure she doesn't suspect me. I'll bring Cody in with me next week or a couple of the gals from Don's Place. There's got to be a group around. Easy enough. Stupid bitch.

I need some cash. Cash! Those kids, they're dirty and hungry! Disgusting. Not my fault. Stupid shit mother. I should send them down to one of their big sister's. Amber—She can look after them for a while. She's got her own two; she won't mind these few more. I don't need to say how long. It's easy enough just to take them there. They're fine. They don't know any different. She's got video games and toys. They don't need no looking after. They'll be fine. I need a drink.

Vodka. Sharp. Dull me. Cold ice. Sharp. Cruising. Clear feeling all over. Isn't that strange? Cloudy and clear at the same time. What the hell?

Nothing to think about. Nothing. Get rid of it all. Moving. Stop moving. Go on and stop.

STILL

1.

I felt the airplane touch down on the tarmac, my body spasming from the unexpected jolt, rubber briefly but instantly burning off of the wheels with a loud roar. It is strange to dream while flying. Looking through the small window, I saw the airport terminal in the distance through a sort of murky haze that dreams produce in vision. It is strange to dream while flying. In the surprising space of involuntary or quiescent memory of sleep, for some reason the airport, though not at all similar, reminded me of the terminal in Ulaanbaatar, arriving as I did there after midnight many years ago, with its incomparable red neon letters lighting up *Chinggis Khaan* atop the sole, minute building, with several of the letters burnt out so that the whole thing produced the effect simultaneously of being endearing and ominous, ambitious and ridiculous, humorous and depressing.

Bandaranaike International Airport is 22 miles north of Colombo. Swami Rock was frighteningly close, and I could feel the energy inside of me beginning at the core and striking out like a hot fire radiating in all directions.

Though I never touched it, thought of it or somehow even placed it, I knew the key was there. I could sense that it was carefully wrapped in the satchel lying against my protruding belly in a wide band with a small purse attached that ran around my entire waist.

Time moved casually, and I felt the bumping of the uneven runway, as we sped along, though seeming not to move at all, onto the adjacent paths until we were suddenly disembarking through what my perception produced as a soft-edged, dim tunnel, my body moving slowly, cumbersome like trying to run in water. Seeing myself from the outside but, strangely, also experiencing the physical sensations internally, I felt the beads of sweat run down the whole length of my face forming at the roots of the hair above my forehead down off my chin, and I also saw them like a cascading waterfall pouring over me. I could feel the nausea permeating me, creating a sense of anxiety inside and outside of sleep. It came from a variety of sources. I was not alone.

*****

It is strange to dream of flying.

*****

My mother is manifest in me. My mother birthed ten children, and I was the ninth. She birthed ten children and ten deaths and also her own death, which came two years ago. I am the last daughter of my mother's to have a child, and I am now having a child. I carry the two fruits: my child and her death and also my own fruit that is my death.

The viceroy came to find me to connect me first to a lost desire and second to the comfort of my missing mother's love. I am waiting to birth my daughter, and I am waiting to know what it means to be part of something, to be part of the world and to create something that is also beyond it. She is the origin of vermilion, the blood and red clay of the earth, of imagination into life of life into art and back into the earth.

Exceptionally, Turner once painted in words, telling us this origin is the very love of painting and music.

> *In days that's past beyond our ken*
> *When Painters saw like other men*
> *And Music sang the voice of truth*
> *Yet sigh'd for Painting's homely proof*
>
> *Her modest blush first gave him taste*
> *And chance to Vermilion gave first place*
> *As snails trace o'er the morning dew*
> *He thus the lines of beauty drew*

Those far faint lines Vermilion dyed
With wonder view'd—enchanted cried

Vermilions honors mine and hence to stand
The Alpha and Omega in a Painters hand

2.

When we think about history, are we able to measure the distances between one age and another, or does it all collapse into one still and timeless moment? Events and figures overlapping each other, occupying the same space, all voices rising in a cacophonous chorus, reliving their bliss their nightmare and presence without cease. When I try to imagine Wagner composing *Tristan und Isolde*, I unconsciously present myself with a picture, an image, an element of my imagination to regard. I cannot see him frantically scribbling any more than I can hear the music, once it is written and performed, of my mind's eye. What I see instead is an image of him writing, hunched over a beautifully crafted, dark mahogany desk, his wife intricately embroidering on a nearby worn ottoman, a somber handmaid watering the heavy rosebush through the open window. What I hear is an image of an orchestra poised at the moment of absolute animation, the conductor with arms suspended overhead, fingers splayed, baton aimed crookedly toward the sky, facial muscles tense, hair standing wildly, gaze fixed on the violins, the audience enraptured, their hands gripping armrests or properly folded in laps with knuckles clenched under white gloves.

Susan Sontag says the same for the movies, claiming that memories of a film amount to *an anthology of a single shot*. Even the interview of Sontag herself, I imagine as a picture—two people in chairs somewhere undefined, floating in a dark space, faces indistinct, thick dark hair with one fat streak of grey. *I can recall the story, lines of dialogue, the rhythm. But what I remember visually are selected moments that I have, in effect, reduced to stills.* Memory operates through the stillness of images, moments, which are part of a continuum, in stasis, halted, unmoving. Why? I think it is because the continuum is not a progression as we might imagine, and so there is no actual propulsion within it but an endless and infinitely minute—imperceptible and undefinable—repetition of instances.

It might seem that we use art to represent the process of breaking down the world into these digestible instances, unable really to apprehend the world in its constant flux, but if we try to remove ourselves from this limited view onto the world, we might see that the flux itself is an infinite, open, perpetual happening in space and time, or rather out of space and time as we know it.

If, as Mitchell writes, the visual arts are a metaphor *for the shaping of language into formal patterns that 'still' the movement of linguistic temporality into a spatial, formal array,* then this suggests that our memory, our mind's eye, uses the tool of stilling in order to process, to understand something, to make it into language. It demonstrates how we must dissect the elements of our perception, of our world, in order to understand them within the framework of language. This is how we see the world.

Murray Krieger explains that 'still' can be understood as an adjective, adverb, and verb to show a *still movement* (*a quiet, unmoving movement*), the act of *still moving* (*forever-now, unending movement*), and *the stilling of movement* (*the quieting of movement and its perpetuation*). The first two are the most commonplace, and the third is a combination of those first two: *a movement that is still and that is still with us.* However, I think the stilling of movement might be an unfortunate or false way of trying to comprehend the world around us. In fact, all of the forms of still are fabrications. There is no silence. There is a cacophony of constant voices all twisting and turning, screaming and singing. There is no stop-motion. There is perpetual movement but without progression. It is as without space and so does not move. It is the third, the collapsing of stillness itself with its constant moving, the forever-now. *L'ici-maintenant.*

3.

When you are born, there is always already a set of complex circumstances swirling about you that is unanticipated, unexpected, but always taken as known, as real, as what the world is. Living is automatic, and whatever you are given in your life, before you have the ability to distinguish what it is that you have and what it is that you don't have and what it is that is there hurting you and what it is there that is loving you, you are simply given a world that is yours. Often times, it is not until you are an adult that you realize how different your world is from that of anyone else. The way you eat, the way your mother treats you or leaves you, the way you hurt or don't hurt, bathe or don't bathe, cry or don't cry, work, play, run, climb, sleep, build space rockets out of toilet paper tubes and aluminum foil, put on a new, winter coat when you're seven and walk out of the dime store as quickly and inconspicuously as possible because mom said.

Somewhere along the line, you learn the difference between right and wrong, and, even if your family does things that are the only way it is known to you, you are still capable of understanding them. If mom stole food, I knew it was wrong, but it was my mom and so I did not question it. She fed us in the way that she knew how. She fed us with stolen food (what fit in her purse), welfare food (powdered milk with water), food from work (frozen fish and chips), food from the dumpsters (bread and doughnuts) and sometimes she didn't feed us at all. Sometimes she didn't come home for days. I am not sure I was ever able to understand that in relation to other children around me, but we do eventually learn how to compare our lives with other children and what we see them receiving, how they are being treated, that it mattered to their parents if they were fed, had lunch money, had clean clothes and winter boots that didn't leak and need plastic bread bags on the inside.

There are so many paths, and the ones that are unacceptable, less acceptable, somehow there is something there to reach out to, that always reaches back.

I'm at the point where, like Rilke says, *ich lerne sehen*. I'm learning to see. There is a well in me. A well that has for so long felt both empty and full. Emptied by the tremendous pouring of emotions into an abyss. Full of the longing, of the love itself, of the desire to express. We relay events as we remember them, as they stick to us, as they are memories. As we recreate them to relive them to make them something new out of the old, which never really was real – but there is great excitement in breaking down life into snapshots. We devour it with considerable heartiness.

4.

I had read it just two days ago in the French press that the old man had died in his sleep. His obituary mentioned the legacy of his father and of his own service at the library over six decades. The news mentioned the cause of death as natural. He had been 87. He left no relatives.

I should have expected this, and maybe I did.

I learned from the obituary that his father had fought in World War I for the French Foreign Legion. He was stationed first in Indochina and later wounded at the Battle of the Somme. He was in Paris at the Armistice and went on to earn a degree from the prestigious Ecole du Louvre. The old man's father returned to Asia as an archeologist, met his future wife and in the late 1920s had his only child. Like Mumtaz Mahal, Anne More, my mom's mom and many others, his wife died in childbirth. He and his son returned to France shortly after, where he took up research service at the Bibliothèque Nationale. He was responsible for the library acquiring several precious artifacts from Indochina. He also died of natural causes and too was approaching 90.

The old man followed nearly identically in his father's footsteps. Though he was born abroad, he was raised by his father in Paris and also studied at the Ecole du Louvre, returning to Southeast Asia where he was part of the archeological recoveries of 1956 in Sri Lanka that included one of the legendary lingam of Shiva. He again returned to Paris, though never marrying, and took up a research position at the library, and is also credited with bringing several notable artifacts with him.

The key, naturally, is not mentioned. I am not sure why I would have expected otherwise. Some vague hope of a clue. It seemed to have always remained a private possession. This leaves its origin as uncertain as ever to me, since it is unclear whether or not the key was recovered in the Orient during the mid-20th Century or if it came from elsewhere, and I also must recall how the description at the library noted its possible European origin. Nevertheless, that does not preclude an origin at Swami, considering the history of the region particularly during the period in which the key seems to have been acquired.

The old man evidently knew he was in possession of something extraordinary. But to what end? All these years? How did it affect him? I imagine he may have felt relief when he found the moment to pass it on, or pass on the message that it contained or will contain or provide. Black Elk shows us that life is all messages and connections across time whether evident or not, deliberate or not, beneficial or harmful or not. *Wherever the truth of vision comes upon the world, it is like a rain*, and I think that when the key finds where it belongs it will be just like that.

5.

When I was born, my mother could not care for me. She was in prison. She gave birth to me in the hospital and was returned to prison three days later. She had ten children and could not care for them, not in the way that children need, and so she tried to commit secret crimes, but these crimes were never really secret and just made her ever more unable to care for her children. When I was born, she was in prison until I was walking, and when I was a child, she was in prison again until I was a girl, and when she was let out, she ran from her new offenses and was gone until I was a woman. I saw her again ten years later, and she was old and worn and broken and had been living in a van and had been abused and had abused herself and lived by alcohol to keep her moving. She died from that soon after, and her body, it was cremated and divided among her ten children.

She died in Montana alone with the death rattle. The last time I saw her was not long before, and my sisters and I whisked her off in a borrowed wheel chair to the local casino, a dark, windowless cavern, walls peppered in bright, singing lights.

There was a stale smoky coating tangible in the air, stale chips, hard candies cemented to one another and homemade, greasy brownies in plastic wrap on a card table in the center of the room. The bodies of the patrons melded with their machines in a blurred, numbing orgy of nickels, wheels and flashing buttons. We sat on torn vinyl swivel chairs fixed to the carpeted floor, staring into soulless spinning windows of cherries, numbers, jokers, queens and fool's gold promises. Old soda and booze on everyone's breath and under their eyelids. Staring, glossed over, waiting, pulling, pressing, a drop of a coin, three coins, no coins. I was there and my mom there and I was with my mom there. I rested my head on her shrunken shoulder as the glow danced around us. My breath fell on her collar and on her neck and in her wiring hair. I buried myself in a space that did not answer back. She gazed undirected toward the machine. My heart beat against her arm, hers inside the machine. Our bodies touched untogether, hair roped like marble, colors unmixed, grey blue eyes, soft noses, loose and pursed lips, flesh of another.

6.

The Koneswaram temple of Trincomalee was built atop Swami Rock as early as in the 6th Century before the Common Era, or even the 16th Century before the Common Era, according to an ancient Tamil poet. Its gopuram columns were added in the 5th Century of the Common Era by Kulakkottan, descendent of Manu Needhi Cholan, legendary Chola king of the Tamil dynasty who upheld justice, it is said, by killing his own son for retribution to a cow whose calf he had trampled under his chariot.

The Chola Empire is responsible for the widespread construction of a certain variety of temples that exist across modern-day India and Sri Lanka and ruled in various forms and sizes over southeast India and Asia from the 3rd Century before the Common Era until the 13th Century of the Common Era, reaching as far north as the Ganges and as far as the Timor Sea to the south. We know that the Koneswaram temple was revered for centuries until its destruction in the 17th Century, and it is thought even that the worship of Eiswara is the most ancient form of worship existing, as it is still a place of pilgrimage and holiness.

There is a massive crevice in the rocks next to the old temple offering a direct view to the sea nearly 400 feet below. It has crudely been dubbed Lovers Leap, in acknowledgment of the dismay of the daughter of the Dutch Sergeant Major Hendrik Adriaan van Rheede, Francina, who, at the end of the 17th Century, allegedly cast herself off the cliff when her lover left her behind.

The story is told that as his ship pulled away from the island, she waited until the moment when it passed directly in view of the precipice before flinging herself toward the sea. Her father erected a memorial to her, but there are several versions to the story including one that claims she did not die at all.

It seems rather that a story was constructed, and subsequent information was unearthed that conflicts with that story, and therefore there are now several possibilities as to what actually took place, although none of them is wholly accurate since the collective data is inherently conflicting. I mean by *conflicting* that the pieces of information that circulate do not comprise one story because all of the elements do not make a coherent whole. It cannot be the case that Lady Francina died and didn't die.

If Lady Francina did not die after casting herself off the rocks, why her father built the existent memorial to her remains unclear. One version of the story surmises that she did jump but survived; another suggests she married a different fellow many years later, after her recovery. According to certain sources and historical records, it has been said that Lady Francina ultimately did not perish but was married several years later likely, it appears to me (though also in conflict with the disparate stories), to the same man who supposedly left her behind—likely because the man who left her and the one she married were both described as a captain of the Dutch East India Trading Company. After her first husband died in 1693 she remarried Anthony Karel van Panhuys, son of Bartholomeusz van Panhuys, a Lord, thus giving her the title of Lady.

In 1929 there was printed the *Journal of the Dutch Burgher Union in Ceylon*, which states in the footnotes by the editor that Francina first married Maurits Cesar de la Boye, Captain in the East India Company Service. It also states that she outlived her father, and therefore *some other explanation would therefore have to be found for the monument*, which unfortunately is not given.

When we learn stories, and when we learn history, we try to make sense of the information we're given by piecing it together to form a whole. Sometimes the process is so fine-tuned that it goes unnoticed. The information comes from disparate sources; it develops over time; we learn parts here and there, and we construct and make sense of the collective story using the model of what we thought was the truth as given to us, before each subsequent piece of information invaded the narrative that has been constructed or is being constructed, or that is always in the process of being constructed or remembered and carried forward. If there is a rupture in the narrative, we question not only its validity but the validity of the entire story, as we've presented it to ourselves or as it was presented to us as something cohesive and true. The process in some ways makes us have expectations that we are not aware of and that sometimes violate our reasoning skills. We are often not aware that we are accepting or reasoning through the elements as we learn them. We take them for whole, and when there are ruptures, the whole permanently fragments.

7.

James Emerson Tennent was an Irish politician who became colonial secretary to Ceylon in 1845. During his five-year term, he wrote two major texts, an account of Christianity in Ceylon and a two-volume encyclopedic study of the island, covering everything from geography and geology to history, religion and politics to the arts and commercial trade. In documenting the geography of Ceylon, Tennent came upon the legend of Pannoa, which he calls *one of the most graceful* perhaps because of its outcome. According to *Ceylon: An Account of the Island, Physical, Historical, and Topographical with Notices of its Natural History, Antiquities and Productions,* Pannoa and neighboring Pannaham, both near the southern edge of the Batticaloa on the eastern coast, are named after the Tamil words *palen-nagai,* Tennent explains, which mean 'smiling babe'.

Tennent writes of an oracle that had foreseen a king of the Deccan Plateau overthrown by his own kin, and so his newborn daughter was cast upon a river lying atop the bark of a sandelwood tree. She did not perish in the water but instead was found afloat on the shores of Ceylon, and adopted by a king, where she eventually herself reigned. The story continues that a Hindu prince was made aware that the rock of Trincomalee, lying in the domain of the young princess, was in fact of the golden and majestic mountain of Meru that had been hurled south by the gods, and so he set upon Ceylon, erecting there a temple to Siva. The princess prepared her army, but on encountering the prince, she instead married him, and upon her death many years later, in his grief he was turned into a golden lotus upon the lingam of Siva in the temple at Swami Rock.

First referenced in the ancient Purana texts, the Koneswaram temple itself, known first as *Koneiswara Parwatia* and allegedly built by the prince of the Pannoa legend, was famously called the Temple of a Thousand Columns. Cholan Kullakottan first sailed to Trincomalee, compelled by the holiness of the temple, and, accordingly, had three further Hindu temples built on its compound, all of which were destroyed by the Portuguese during the Thirty Years' War there at Swami Rock, including the incredible *Koneiswara Parwatia*. In his 1895 account, Tennent proclaims that the remaining edifice that is contained within the compound of Fort Frederick is still known as the Temple of a Thousand Columns, though only small echoes of its original grandeur remain, including minor engravings, among them a prophesy claiming that the land would be ruled for 500 years by Westerners beginning the 17th Century, after which time it will revert to the Northerners.

Hunter, fly fisherman and all around sportsman, Philip K. Crowe, author of *Sport Is Where You Find It* (1953), subsequently wrote *Diversions of a Diplomat* in 1956 to account for his own time spent as American Ambassador to Ceylon in the 1950s. Crowe claims that the pillar on which is written the memorial for Lady Francina is the only remaining such pillar to have belonged to the Temple of a Thousand Columns, or Aayiram Kaal Mandapam.

Peculiarly, Crowe's explanation and details of the Pannoa legend, the precise account of the name derivations, and the very style of his writerly word choice are strikingly similar to Tennent's, so much so that they are, in fact, often exact. Information belongs to no one, but somehow words do. When an author borrows another's words and claims them as their own without acknowledging rightful ownership, it is considered plagiarism. In the case of mythology, folklore and legends, certainly it is impossible to ascertain an original voice, and so such words and even texts are borrowed without qualm. I can't help but wonder if Crowe thought Tennent's writings on the subject were somehow archaic enough as not to matter any longer, but to the extent either that no one would notice or mind that he was copying them word for word.

The collecting and retelling of one another's stories, using one another's words, sharing ideas and voices in the constant swirl of information and its dissemination makes it difficult to decipher, or even to comprehend, what ideas and elements belong to whom and why and how they belong. As we partake in the web of one and another and the greater experience of our intricacies, all of the bodies, moments, details, breaths, senses and perceptions, we ask ourselves what the value or circumstance or consequence is of violating, and seeking to call violation on, the placement of words on the tongue, the mutual thoughts or the weak, nascent or even unclever thoughts that are then allegedly stolen.

253

Aggregating ideas is the collective experience that defines us, constitutes us before we were born, before we knew into what we were being born and what would grow in us as we grew into the skin holding our insides in place. We are also broken apart as a unity through the individual experiences that we undertake, whether that is in action, in voice, in all of our senses. We protect that morsel of identity. We guard it. We cherish it, and rightly so, but we also allow it to be absorbed, and we contribute with it to the greater collective, in action, in voice, in all of our senses.

8.

I was going through some of my belongings, and I discovered some old home movies in a long-forgotten box from my childhood, maybe ten or twenty two-minute reels. I went out and rented a projector for the weekend, which one can do inexpensively, and I watched them against a sheet that I tucked on top of the door before closing it. Most but not all of the films are of my older brothers and sisters before me, before the last three of us ten were even born. The machine was loud and reminded me of when I had first seen these films when I was maybe ten years old, watching those films while back in America during mom's trial and sentencing, these films when I was maybe two and even smaller. The way the images flicker, and once in a while the reel gets stuck and makes that crazy clicking sound, the edges of the moment in real life are faded and scratched. In one particular film, we have taken a vacation somewhere looks like in Florida, and my father is maneuvering a pontoon boat. The film moves first from him at the wheel, then the lot of us running around on the deck of the flat boat, until we notice the camera and begin to smile. The reel ends with me waving into the shot. As I watched it, I felt compelled to wave back and did.

9.

150 kilometers in from the coast on the mainland, at the point at which the small islands between Ceylon, or Sri Lanka, and the mainland are the greatest, is the Meenakshi Temple, which also contains a Hall of a Thousand Columns, though it actually contains only 985 carved pillars. Its name is strangely misleading.

In its precision of design, the temple permits the viewer to see from any angle a straight line along any row of the columns. Though Ariyanatha Mudaliar had the hall constructed in 1569, just several decades before the Thirty Years' War, it did not suffer the same fate as the temple at Trincomalee in 1622 and remains standing today. The complex of Meenakshi Temple is itself of a far more ancient origin, though its original structures were destroyed multiple times in its long history, including during the Thirty Years' War. Along with a dozen other south Indian temples, it is also home to the Musical Pillars, consisting of five large pillars that are in turn comprised of 22 smaller pillars, each carved out of a single stone and each of which produce a distinct tone when struck.

Meenakshi Temple has a *swayambu* lingam—a naturally-forming monolith, as opposed to those manmade, usually small, cylindrical, stone objects, to serve in shrines to Shiva. Legend tells of Indra, god of rain and thunder, journeying on a wearying pilgrimage when he found his sufferings to begin to ease as he came upon the swayambu lingam. He erected the Meenakshi Temple and enshrined the lingam within it, where it still remains.

The counterpart to the lingam is the yoni, a flat stone with an open center and that often serves as a sort of placement receptacle for the lingam. Together the lingam and yoni represent creation through the indivisible union of the two becoming one.

10.

I turned the satchel that the old man gave me over in my hand without opening it but feeling the hard contents tumble around inside, the bottom of the soft pouch molding to the shape within. As I held the slender, metal object in my palm through the fabric of the satchel, I suddenly had the idea that Arthur C. Clarke's interest in learning scuba diving in Sri Lanka may have directly resulted from knowing, not only that the ruins of the Koneswaram Temple lay on the sea floor, but that significant artifacts had precisely recently been discovered in 1950 that pointed to the possibility for further, massive discoveries potentially in the near future. Clarke knew those ruins were down there, and he knew they needed to be found, once the world had learned that original shrines to Shiva, made of precious metals and various types of statues of other gods, were found buried 500 meters from the site of the old Koneswaram Temple, having been simply stumbled upon by the local urban council as they dug for a water well. So it was true, or rather, this is how the discovery of their continued existence was made: precious objects were spared universal destruction as priests and pilgrims hid them in the earth as quickly as they could, before themselves facing massacre, as the temples were swiftly destroyed one after another during the fateful siege in 1622.

In his subsequent dives, Clarke also found one of the legendary swayambu lingams, said originally to have come from Tibet and brought to Koneswaram by the mythological King Raavan.

In the *Ramayana*, the century-old epic, King Raavan, or Ravana, is an antagonistic figure who rides the birdlike Wilmana, or Vimana, which, in Sanskrit vimāna denotes the concept of a length of measure, or a bridge across something, and so it is used to mean anything from palace and temple to flying machine to more metaphorical definitions including the medical reference for measurement and a literary text for religious inspiration. In the Sanskrit epics, vimāna usually refers to flying chariots pulled by great animals, such as King Ravana's notorious bird figure, which is the first flying vimana in Hindu mythology.

This kind of connection brings to my mind the recent research in biolinguistics that has shown intimate links between the development of birdsongs, artificial intelligence and human infant babbling. Notwithstanding the lack of information on psycholinguistics, it seems that human language is learned, on the acoustic level, much in the same way that birds learn their songs, namely through understanding the links between transitions in grammar. The breakthrough component comes from unveiling the manner in which entire grammar sequences are immediately understood once the transitions between the syllables, of either the word or song, are understood. There is no trial and error but an immediate grasp of the entire sequence that constitutes the word or song, though this discovery itself is painstaking and lengthy. A recent study suggests that babies move from *bababa* to *babadaga*, for example, at the moment when *daga* rolls of the tongue and not through the exercise of attempting a repetition of the two parts together.

The theory of generative grammar rests on the belief that there is a biological necessity of the grammars of languages. It postulates that language is created and operational based on syntax, on the idea that the individual parts of language have independent values that are uniquely acquired and understood through an innate human ability to place them within a kind of comprehensive language structure. The goal of generative grammar is to investigate how infants move from no language whatsoever to complete language within a limited period of primary language input, by using that observational fact as the pretext for grounding the theory. Noam Chomsky developed this branch of linguistics in the 1960s, which relies on the notion of the *poverty of the stimulus*, which is the idea, in observing the limitations of children, again in terms of time and input, that natural language grammar cannot be learned and therefore an innate mechanism, or universal grammar, must be at play that makes natural language learning possible.

A more recent development in generative grammar is the field of construction grammar, which posits that the grammatical construction—any syntactic string of words together with its semantic and pragmatic elements (form beyond syntax including phonological qualities, content beyond semantics including pragmatics)—is the primary unit of language and not simply the syntactic unit, such that, as George Lakoff contends in his ground breaking work in the 1970s, the *meaning of the whole is not a function of the meanings of the parts*, as with traditional Chomskyan generative grammar. In construction grammar, *the constructions themselves have meaning*; distinguishing it from basic generative grammar based on the syntactic unit: the meaning is not the parts, which are then put together to form syntax. Construction grammar itself has spawned a large family, one branch being fluid construction grammar, created by Luc Steels, which is an operational, computational system that grounds grammars in the sensorimotor experiences of robots.

11.

Two days after she died, we cleaned out mom's storage space—a shoddy little tin can at some cheap, outdoor facility on the outskirts of that small town in Montana; the ten of us children going through her spare
belongings, trudging through an incredible snowstorm
to get there, taking turns sitting in the idling pickup
truck to get warm throughout the long, freezing, snow
white afternoon, throwing most things away, old cook-
books, boxes of sewing bits, dirty clothing, kitchen
supplies, a box of cloth bags for bottles of rum, ancient,
worn-out gadgets, drawings, pieces of newspaper clip-
pings, recipe boxes, a couple horse shoes, objects she
would thought had value but never did, saving whatever odds and ends would be meaningful. We found just
two books: the *Deathbed Edition* of *Leaves of Grass* and
The Complete Works of Edgar Allan Poe. My younger
brother took the Poe. I took the Whitman.

It is impossible to imagine a world that is not infused with this aura, this essence that mom felt and
created and we all felt and cherished and looked towards for meaning and a fullness where otherwise
there wouldn't be any. This supernatural delicacy, this
mystery, this ability she had and gave to us to always
imagine that there is something greater. It was never a
spiritual greatness; it was always a darkness that permeated all things and that touched us unexpectedly, in
no way that could be anticipated. It was graceful and
at the same time disquieting. It was rather unnerving,

mom sometimes talking about the ghost of her brother who died in infancy, and one of my sisters claiming extrasensory abilities and so on, both having me believe that I too had some gift.

12.

Maturin Murray Ballou wrote *The Pearl of India* in 1894 shortly before he died in Cairo. A writer of fiction and nonfiction, Ballou founded *Gleason's Pictorial Drawing-Room Companion*, was first editor of the *Boston Daily Globe* and traveled the world with his wife, writing numerous travel books of their destinations. In the beginning of *The Pearl of India* Ballou describes how his sailing vessel was accompanied by *a score of white-winged, graceful marine birds* that traveled alongside from the Malacca Straits all the way to Ceylon. *It was the very poetry of motion.* The birds seemed to vanish during the night, and even the wisest of seamen did not know where they may have reposed.

Nearly three-quarters of birds migrate long distances, and the lack of sleep they endure, often while crossing large bodies of water, is compensated through their ability to rest simultaneously while flying by keeping one eye open, while the other eye and other half of the brain shut down. This unilateral eye closure allows for a semi-conscious nap in the air, uninterrupted travel and relatively sufficient protection from danger. Other birds employ what researchers call drowsiness, where both eyes are partially closed during the rest period in flight. But these half-awake reprieves last mere seconds and number into the hundreds during a migrating flight of thousands of kilometers. The northern lapwing, for example, flies continuously across the Atlantic at a speed of 150 kilometers per hour, making the complete journey in 24 hours.

The commonly recognizable butterfly known as the Monarch also migrates overwinter, sometimes traveling thousands of miles over the course of three to four generations of its species. A single butterfly, the lifespan of which is two months, cannot live to make the entire journey itself, which may take six months or more. Instead, the butterflies reproduce during the voyage and the final offspring overwinters in the south equatorial destination during a non-reproductive phase of several months. The Monarch is of very few insects that are able to cross the Atlantic Ocean. It remains a mystery how the butterflies of many subsequent generations know where to migrate and overwinter, returning precisely to the same spot, the same trees. The Viceroy butterfly is slightly smaller than the Monarch but completely resembles it in its wing design and coloring, and in this way escapes bird predators who are wary of the poisonous Monarch that eats from the equally poisonous milkweed plant, storing the poison, thus protecting it from birds that become sick and subsequently learn not to repeat the error.

13.

The musical pillars across south India are not hollow. They are enormous, individually-sculpted solid stones, ten to fifteen feet in height, delicately narrow with gradually increasing girth at either end across varying concentric bands with intricate engravings of animals, deities and scenes of antiquity, that reside collectively as 22 or 48, or another number, smaller pillars within or composing each larger pillar supporting it; those two or five, or another number, larger pillars in turns supporting the temple itself. The acoustic system of the musical pillars is a modern marvel. It is not clear how the solid stone pillars are not only able to produce such fantastic acoustics across different scales but how those emanations in turn resemble the sounds of various Indian instruments included stringed, brass and wind. There is another form of musical pillar which is hollow and which has an open cavity into which air can be blown to create the musical resonance. The Musical Pillars are still used during rituals or *pujas*.

The Sthapathis and Shilpis of the Vishwakarma caste are the artisans responsible for the creation and building of the variety of extraordinary Hindu temples. Master craftsmen, they gathered the stones for the musical pillars based on their acoustic quality, where subtle differences indicated into which musical category the pillar would fall and which part of the pujas it would correspond, how it would be used, what its reverberation would signify. Pillars with a metallic sound are used for worship in relation to the female idol, yoni, whereas the stones whose sound resembles the timbre of precious gems are used in the worship characterized with male idols, the lingam. The sound of the musicians tapping the pillars creating harmonics and echo effects with the neighboring pillars resonates throughout the village and valley in which the temple is located.

If all the pillars of one temple are struck simultaneously, a synchronized dissonance is produced sending a delicate warble of glassy voices up toward the sky and out toward the valley that is parallel with the sensation to the eye of a flight of birds pushing wind toward the waves over a darkened, moon-crested ocean, in the stillness of an unanticipating air. The wind draws in the expelled breaths, the warm nostrils draw in the grinding current of melodies.

14.

Through mom, everything became infused with an immaterial presence. Everything—down to the objects lying on the floor, to our dreams at night, to the shape of an old woman's face at the market, to the precise cost of gasoline on the way to the funeral coinciding with the date of mom's birth, to finding pennies on street corners. Superstition, superstition in a way that came not from what we did, not rituals, but things that were affecting us, as we felt them, as we seemed to notice them. It seems mom taught us, unconsciously, indirectly, to believe that the world held something stronger, even more beautiful if also lugubrious—uncontrollable, forever unknowable, untouchable— than anything you could imagine yourself, but you were imagining it yourself, and so the magic failed to empower us but somehow crippled us into thinking there were forces beyond our control, instead of allowing us to recognize that those very same forces are emanating from us; they are us.

*****

I see myself look out over Swami Rock, perhaps standing in the same spot as Lady Francina, gazing into an open sea with nothing obstructing my view with the tide below with the sun high with a vision of myself carrying my daughter and thinking of my poor mother on her deathbed turning pale breathing forced eyes rolling back. We struggle to stay in this world and we struggle to help our children come into this world and we struggle to stay awake and to know and make sense and understand. *The grinding water and the gasping wind*, says Wallace Stevens.

15.

It was thought until only very recently that the Viceroy butterfly is not poisonous in the same way as the Monarch and therefore protects itself by imitating the Monarch, thus risking its life by relying on this natural disguise to keep it from harm. However, it was discovered at the end of the 20th Century that the Viceroy is itself poisonous, though perhaps less so, yet it is thought that some form of mimicry must be taking place if the two distinct butterflies resemble one another in terms of colors and markings but are different sizes, different diets and all the qualities that distinguish different species.

A viceroy rules in place of a monarch, and the butterflies are named in the order of a royal hierarchy because of their resemblance to one another and their size. The Monarch is followed by the Queen butterfly, which has the same markings and is also poisonous but is slightly smaller. The Viceroy is significantly smaller than both the Monarch and the Queen, and though it does not lay its eggs on poisonous milkweed but rather goldenrod, poplar and willow, these plants too have their own poisonous component that is stored by the Viceroy, deterring predators.

16.

I considered the last words that the old man said to me. *It is better to keep your breath cold.* It is from the *Conference of the Birds*, and specifically the poem *Looking for Your Own Face*.

> *So you sigh in front of mirrors*
> *and cloud the surface.*
>
> *It's better to keep your breath cold.*
> *Hold it, like a diver does in the ocean.*
> *One slight movement, the mirror-image goes.*
>
> *Don't be dead or asleep or awake.*
> *Don't be anything.*

I am beginning to understand, I think, that the man with the watch that his sighs, his speaking had clouded the mirror from his sight, from his ability to accept, without penetrating, either the story of the key or the story of himself, of the young woman, of Hein. I too, perhaps anyone, could be victim of this approach, the story of the viceroy, the enchantress, my mother, Hein. And then the next stanza—

> *What you most want,*
> *what you travel around wishing to find,*
> *lose yourself as lovers lose themselves,*
> *and you'll be that.*

The key arrives when it has a role to play. The man with the watch failed the key and was consumed by his own dread, not by Hein but by the fear of Heinlein. His story may have been mine already in the making. It was there that I was to begin with mine. Over the course of our space in time, we encounter the key, not this key but another key, the key for each one of us and follow its mystery until it guides us to the clear space, *the truth of vision*, after the rain.

The key is connected to Simorgh, and that is not a coincidence, but it is also not extraordinary, I know now. I know in all the elements and what seem as co-incidences, what is not hidden from view but by warm breath.

As the baby grows inside, as I move closer to her entering the world, I realize that, despite also coming closer to discovering the purpose of the key, I am aware that it becomes insignificant and something about the entire journey begins to pale as a small diversion or digression in the collective experience.

17.

Mom wanted to be cremated. She had been working as a cook at a truck stop on the edge of town near the interstate in the small Montana town before she died. Toothless and beaten down, old, aching hands serving greasy, gravy-laden chicken-fried steak, wiping down tables with a dirty rag, slowly, painfully hobbling back to the kitchen to fill new orders. Her boss was about to let her go—too many mistakes, too many apologies, too many second chances—when she had to be put in hospice anyway. A month later she was gone.

Mom wanted to give herself to all of us. When each of us was born, she gave us a unique nickname. Mine was Bird.

In the middle of the night, my younger brother and I divided her ashes up into ten soap dispensers from the dollar store that one of our older sisters had picked out. We found rubber stoppers at the hardware store that fit perfectly, replacing the little pump. Mom wanted her ashes distributed among her ten children. We had to do it in the middle of the night, because no one wanted to see the bone and ash and bits that were in the bag. My brother was bravest. He handled the bag. I rotated the dispensers with a funnel for him to fill and kept everything organized. We thought about how to divide her perfectly evenly. I got out measuring cups and then measuring spoons.

My brother poured one cup in each urn, as I moved them down the line on some old newspaper covering the table. We were staying in a motel room in Montana near the university. We would judge how much was left to share out, and then my brother would switch to a smaller measuring tool. Next came the half cup. One by one, he poured, and I held the little urn and funnel, carefully placing a stopper in each one, keeping track of which one had how much already inside. The urns were plastic, cheap and painted a nice color to look like old stone. One had a crack, the plastic was too thin. Good thing we bought an extra. My brother then shifted to the quarter cup, then the tablespoon, then the teaspoon, then a half a teaspoon. Then finally he was eyeing up a quarter teaspoon and an eighth of a teaspoon inside the scoop of the half-teaspoon.

When she was all divided, we carefully wrapped each one in paper and our handcrafted cardboard boxes, so that everyone could take her home the next day, flying back to Ohio or California or Oregon or Washington or Paris. Wrapped in paper and then tissue paper, carefully covered in clear packing tape, then put in a plastic baggy, then finally the little cardboard box. There was mom, for each of us. That's how it ended. That night, with my brother and me, giving her over to each of us.

*****

Do we look for our own face in the face of our mother? Or is it the other way around that she looks for her face in me? I looked at her face and saw death. I look upon the face of my daughter, and what will I see?

18.

It was late and the sun was finishing its descent, enclosed behind the hills, behind the old buildings, washed out from the light turning to amber and silver and ash. We walked over old railroad tracks, and we felt the peace radiating through us knowing as we walked that our journey was full of purpose and creation. The life that we carried within us directed us toward the place where it would come to know the world, and we would be the deliverer. We walked calmly, casually, knowingly, and we walked together with one another as though we were one, as though we were both the same and different, a life and its end, the two fruits of each creation.

I began to feel the pains of the child making its way through my body, and as we walked, I began to feel an urgency to bring my body closer to the earth, to begin the process of unfolding one life out of another, to recognize my own mortality in the life and breath of the one coming out of me with her mortality and her body for giving life. And as we walked, I chose to kneel down, time carried on without pause and without markers but in a long, steady stream as one perpetual moment without beginning or end, and as I kneeled down, the child stirred in me and pushed against me and struggled with me and drew out in one direction and my body and my womb in another with time moving long and slow and still. Before I knelt we chose a shelter where I would pass the life through me, and as we had walked along the rails, we had come upon the old train station that was empty and small and crumbling, and I knelt there, I crouched there at the station in the old telephone booth where the glass was thick and encrusted but still clear, and it is here that Heinlein arrived.

19.

I am the animator. There are moments when I awaken and realize that the dreams which just passed were capable of swallowing me whole and extinguishing all of my efforts, all of my ability to be practical, logical to remember how to carry on. I often feel like I'm about to disappear in my sleep. Goethe writes,

> Der Worte sind genug gewechselt,
> Laßt mich auch endlich Taten sehn!

Words have been sufficiently exchanged, let me finally see action!

20.

At Swami Rock I lose myself as lovers lose themselves and leap off the cliff into the sea. My body begins as a parachute, limbs open then furled becoming a bulleted dive ending as a clustered, irregular ball, unhinged descending. I am swallowed and sink down softly, smoothly into the canal of the earth, with a thickness to the comforting body of water surrounding me, caressing me down to the seabed floor. An ominous temple ruin looms before me, embedded, fixed in the deep blue, buried deep in the sand, organically built into the very bottom of the world; gentle, gliding seaweed, waving in the wind that is waves, slow motion plants from the clay bottom sleepily curling up like starry nights. My arms, legs, torso, swirling hair, everything weightless and detached, move slowly toward an elaborately decorated *prakaram*, former outer courtyard of the temple complex. I reach to my center, to the now loose band surrounding my body and remove the satchel as it lay resting there against my empty belly. It too is weightless, and I see it illuminate, guiding my hand my arm my body toward the door of the prakaram. It slides delicately into the lock. There is no sound, the space is thick like ears full of fresh, padded cotton. There is absence of sound, but I feel the key and lock connect and click. I enter the ruins and float along lost in time lost in a calm as it carries me forward toward the cavernous rooms and inner prakaram and pathways with schools of fish passing through, seahorses and starfish gently rocking to and fro moving with and against, along and counter. I open the next door and once again pass through until I feel myself directed deeper into the labyrinth of corridors and halls, all strewn with green and blue coral climbing the walls the floors the shapes across the space aching until I am at the center and there are no more doors. There is a stone chest rectangle and worn, like a great sunken pirate treasure standing alone, and the key feels ever more weightless as it moves closer. As I pass it there into the final lock, I begin to feel a new kind of lightness, a floating as if in air. My body itself loses its form, and we are looking into the chest with millions of eyes, as millions of eyes are reflected back upon us, upon all of us, there staring into the Eternal Mirror.

* * * * *

KATY MASUGA, University of Paris-Sorbonne recent fellow, is the author of two monographs on Henry Miller, a forthcoming, second novel, *The Blue of Night*, numerous short stories, and two dozen essays and anthology chapters on subjects ranging from altered books to language games to Shakespeare and Company in Paris to the vegetarian diet of Frankenstein's Creature. She holds a doctorate in Comparative Literature and a joint doctorate in Theory and Criticism from the University of Washington, Seattle. *The Origin of Vermilion* is her first novel.